Emma's Run

A Novel

Dianne Zimmermann

Printed in the United States of America by Lightning Source, Inc.

Cover art by the author.

ISBN 978-1-937862-61-9

Library of Congress Control Number 2013918785

Published 2013 by BookCrafters, Parker, Colorado.
SAN-859-6352, BookCrafters@comcast.net

Copies of this book may be ordered from
www.bookcrafters.net and other online bookstores.

Acknowledgements

I would like to thank LA Mott,
Lou Platten and Cynthia Bechtel
for being readers and offering suggestions
and words of encouragement and support.

I dedicate this book to them
as well as all my friends
whose never-ending encouragement
drove me on when the going got tough.

Chapter One

Spring is in the air, balmy breezes stir the gentle mist that illuminates the reflective glow of the streetlights. Emma is feeling especially grateful today and counting her many blessings as she runs along her usual evening route that meanders through tree lined streets. Knowing all too well the familiar terrain: pot holes, curbs and raised sidewalks. She runs on autopilot and allows her mind to wander; as she easily glides up to the hill along the park where through the trees she can see the city skyline. Her heart warms at the sight.

Almost finished with her run, she rounds the block and passes the edge of the park where large beautiful brick homes surrounded by mature oak trees, neatly trimmed lawns and hedges adorn the street. Old fashion streetlights align the way and add to the unique ambiance of the neighborhood. It's no wonder it's a favored location for homes and businesses alike. It's close to the hustle and bustle of downtown yet has a charming small town feel.

This trendy part of the city is located close to universities with teaching hospitals, theaters, and the symphony. It is a part of the city where street-side shops and cafes provide awnings that protect coffee sippers and diners from sudden spring showers. Emma loves the change in seasons and the fresh smell of spring rain in the air. This is the perfect weather for an evening run.

She pulls her cap down to shield her eyes from the mist that is now turning into light rain. It is a refreshing rain, and she is close enough to the end of her run that she does not mind getting wet.

Emma, a fit young sixty year old, easily runs up and down the area's steep hills, skipping over curbs, dodging puddles and jumping up onto sidewalks. Her silver, almost white, shoulder length hair is tied back through the opening in her cap. The light rain dampens and caresses her cheeks and accentuates her lovely complexion giving her classic model looks a glow. Her slender athletic figure easily moves in the latest style reflective running gear and can be seen from all directions. Emma is one to take advantage of the safety visibility that reflectors can bring. She is supercharged this spring-like evening and darts with quickened pace, accuracy and agility. The winter as been long and hard and like the tree buds glistening with renewed freshness, Emma is ready to break out and feel the rebirth of spring along with her daily running stress release.

Chapter Two

Raised by strict Catholic parents with high expectations, Emma attempted to please and to excel at everything she took on. She never colored outside the lines, always, tried her best, respected her family's wishes and never wanted to do anything to upset or embarrass them. Being the only child the pressure was all on her. Her parents were old school and strict and raised Emma to respect authority and social guidelines. From early on when Emma had crushes on girls, rather than boys, she thought nothing of this; that is, not until the other girls at school flirted and chased after boys. Then with a hopeless sinking feeling in her stomach, she realized that she was different. Afraid, she hid the emotions she felt. She hid those feelings deep down with her soul. She told herself that she was not different, that being fond of a best friend was normal. She was confused and afraid to talk to anyone for fear of being ridiculed, ostracized and disappointing to her parents. After all it wasn't that long ago when homosexuals were institutionalized, giving lobotomies, shock treatments, and medicines to cure homosexuality. The church setting the rules of behavior for society condemned homosexuality.

Emma's heart ached, and she was confused. It was socially comfortable to date men, but her heart longed for the touch of a woman. When she was with her boyfriend, Charles; she felt like a woman. She felt that she fit in, and besides her parents liked him.

Being old fashioned, her parents wanted her safe and protected in marriage even though they never seemed to get along themselves and appeared to be unhappy. In the bookstore, her parents put on a happy face, but in private they argued all the time. No matter that they were unhappy, they still thought that Emma needed a man to provide and look after her. And, of course, they wanted grandchildren so being the only child the pressure was all on her.

Sometimes the expectations were too many, and that is why she began running. She ran to calm the constant pressure she felt with the fact that her future was laid out in front of her. She and she alone would inherit the bookstore her parents owned, and she and her husband would run the business. Charles was an aspiring accountant, so he was perfect for the task, and her parents liked his friendly, warm personality.

Emma thought that pleasing others would please her. And that life could be so much easier if she went with the flow of the church, her parents, and acceptable social norms. And as with running, that life has its steep hills, and bumps in its path; but she could get through them.

Chapter Three

The void Emma was feeling was filled, when Bob introduced her to Alice. It happened when Emma and Charles went out one evening with Charles' friend Bob and his girlfriend, Alice. Emma was instantly attracted to Alice and felt that they had been together in a past life. The strong attraction was so vivid that it scared Emma, but she had never felt more at home. It seemed that Charles had somehow sensed the possible connection between Emma and Alice and suggested they double date.

"Her name is Alice; you'll like her," Charles had eagerly suggested. "In fact, she reminds me a lot of you," he added. "I think that you two could become good friends, like Bob and I have."

He was right; how well he knew her. Oddly enough he saw something in her that she couldn't see in herself, probably because she was so conditioned with parental and cultural messages.

Charles was correct in his prediction; Emma and Alice did hit it off and became fast friends. The hidden truth was that Emma was immediately smitten. They say opposites attract; Emma had to disagree in her case. It was rather like looking in a mirror when it came to their personalities and things they both enjoyed. They had the same sense of humor, same taste in clothes and loved hanging out and going shopping together. They even had the same taste in hairstyles, and boyfriends. They were the perfect four-some.

It was a perfect world indeed. Emma felt content and was soon forgetting about her parents and the pressures of social "norms" and expectations. She felt free to love, and allowed herself to feel vulnerable enough to be loved.

****

From her earliest recollection, Emma watched and listened to her parents fight. She sat next to them at church and listened to the sermons where the priest barked orders, begged for money, and condemned the hedonist. It seemed to Emma that anything pleasurable was a sin. And that women did not have the same power or social status that men had. Women and girls were taught to be docile, and subservient. Men were considered smarter and stronger. Even at a young age it depressed Emma when she realized that priest drank beer, smoked cigars and that the nuns took a vow of poverty and had to scrape by on donations.

Emma came from a generation where men were taught to be tough and raised not to show their emotions. Asking her mother why, her mother responded, "Well, so men are tough enough to fight in wars." Even as a child searching for the reasoning of these social ideals, Emma could not grasp that concept and thought that if men were taught not to be so rough and tough, maybe there would not be so many wars.

As a young girl, Emma saw the double standards of men and it saddened her. She envied men. She wanted the same job and education and active sports advantages that they had - to be encouraged and free to explore the world, to be able to travel on her own without fear, and to make her own decisions. There was a time when a woman couldn't get a home loan or get financing on a car. Job opportunities were limited. Job listings in the newspaper were in men and women's categories. For women: Librarians, teachers, nurses, telephone operators, clerks and secretaries. Remarkably enough women who did work at decent paying jobs remained single and were called spinsters or Old Maids to be socially pitied. The price a single woman paid for loving her independence. No young women wanted to be labeled an Old Maid, so marriage was encouraged at a young age. Women were paid very little because bosses and men in general felt a woman's place was in the home taking care of the family. Wages for women were low, about half or less of what a man made because society in general thought all women should be housewives and that the husband, as head-of-household was the main breadwinner in the family and made enough to support the whole family.

As a young girl and not fitting in with liking boys and wanting to be married, Emma should have realized then that she was a lesbian, but she had no role models and thought this was a phase that would pass.

Chapter Four

It wasn't about words or description when it came right down to it; it was what was going on in her mind and her heart. Her heart would melt at the sight of Alice, her blonde hair and blue eyes. She longed to hold her close to her heart. She could easily give and accept love with Alice touching, holding, and feeling. This is what life is all about she thought. Time stood still when they were together. Of course, like any relationship, feelings change and the infatuation, the crush, can wear with time and the toils and demands of everyday life.

****

Emma daydreams as she runs, thinking of the past as she nears the street where she happily lives in very pleasant surroundings above the bookstore with Alice. Yes, they did eventually get together. But there were times when Emma felt that after all these years that true intimacy was missing and that Alice withdrew into her own quiet world, and she wanted the Alice from the days of long ago. Or was this Emma's way of facing life, to look at the dark side. If things are too good, then taking them for granted or feeling that love surely will end and subconsciously push it away only to want it back when it is too late, and the emotional damage had been done.

****

Emma remembers when their relationship became sexual many years ago. It was one dizzying beer-drinking night out at a local pub. Alice was flirting with her. It was like a dare, just how far can we go with this? After pizza and a few beers that gave her courage, Alice invited Emma to her place. Sitting ever so close on the couch, laughing, teasing, a kiss is stolen. A shy smile exchanged and then more kisses, deeper kisses, touching, exploring. One kiss led to another and more, they ended up spending the night together wrapped in each other's arms. It was total bliss. Emma had never felt this way before, certainly not this way about Charles. She felt no betrayal where Charles was concerned, for this was too far out of the realm of normal reality. Emma was blown away by how magical she felt. This, whatever it was with Alice, was in a total different category of wonderment and magical delight. She felt an intense desire for Alice and was able to give as well as receive affection, something she had never felt with Charles. She realized she was not sexually attracted to him as she was to her amazement and delight, with Alice.

A new world of possibilities had opened up to her; a new way of thinking of how the world should be at being more open to diversity and differences. It made her realize that she had prejudices against homosexuality only because she didn't understand and was gay herself. She had often heard and now concurred, that what we fear or hate most about others may indeed lie buried deep within our own inner core, our very soul.

****

What happened back then, she wondered now as she ran in the light mist? Peer pressure? Was it just too hard to face, to handle, not living the straight life. Charles and Bob had began questioning their relationship, hinting with jokes about them being together all the time, and making odd remarks about them becoming lesbians. They should have just dumped the guys and loved each other; however, at the moment, neither of them was ready to face the challenges of coming out, and staying in good graces with their families seemed a more significant issue.

Eventually, they began to see less and less of each other, each finally marrying their boyfriends. Although Emma and Alice were lovers, neither wanted to face the personal and social difficulties of a lesbian lifestyle.

And now Emma regretted all the time that she and Alice had missed. All the opportunities they had of being together, if only there weren't influenced by outside pressures. Never the less, social norms led them to stray apart, ignoring the love they felt for each other. But love Emma's love for Alice ran deep and even while

Emma was with Charles, she fantasized about Alice and missed her warm soft touch.

****

Oh yes Emma and Alice got married, just not to each other — to Charles and Bob. Their ceremony was lovely and sweet. They had a small double wedding. However romantic it appeared, the wedding was bittersweet, instead of being her spouse, Alice was her maid of honor and Alice's husband to be, Bob, Charles best man. They shared mutual friends and all four had fairly small families, so it worked out as far as guests and attendants were concerned. The setting was rather lovely. They were married in a park; the brides-to-be rode in horse-drawn carriages along the lake up through the oak trees to the white ribbon, and various varieties of white flower bouquets that filled the pavilion where the grooms and groomsmen waited. The men wore black tuxedos with tails and top hats and the bridesmaids wore gowns the color of pastel orchids. A small string quartet played. It was lovely, and it was so wrong because both women had feelings for each other and confessed as much to each other right before the wedding, but all the plans were made, and there was the stigma. Neither was ready to admit to the world that they were lesbians. Plans were made, the wedding party of college friends and families were invited. Invitations were mailed, and gifts were already arriving, there simply was no backing out.

They just have to grin and bear it. Well, it wasn't all that bad for there was lots of partying and fun times fitting in with the ever accepting norms of society. Besides, it would be so much easier just to be married, and they could continue seeing each other intimately and no-one would be the wiser. Right?

****

But matters of the heart are difficult to hide, and Emma's marriage to Charles grew rocky with time. Charles was romantic and more giving before they married but then over time it seemed he became controlling. Wanting to know her whereabouts and wanting to know her every move every minute of the day. Did he suspect? Did he know that she and Alice secretly engaged in romantic and loving afternoon sexual delight?

After a time, Emma and Alice grew tired of the secrecy and wanted more. They wanted to be together every day and every night. Alice wanted to leave Bob, but Emma would not leave Charles. Her parents were very fond of him, and it would have disappointed them. They wouldn't have understood. They were getting on in years, and it would have crushed them.

Not to be able to be free with their love took its toll and she and Alice soon argued more and made love less. After a time, they drifted apart, that is until one day years later when Alice happened by the bookstore that Emma now ran by herself after her parents died and she had divorced Charles.

Chapter Five

For years, Emma had been unhappy, for the church, gender roles, and cultural stigma kept most folks in moral disarray. Shame was a powerful tool. Emma grew unhappy because Charles withdrew and was seldom home. Emma had her suspicions and thought that Charles may have been involved in some shady real estate dealings. He became secretive and condescending when she asked him questions about his business.

"Don't worry your pretty little head over it," he commanded as if she weren't capable of understanding the difficulties of the big business world. It was a man's world after all.

****

Emma thought that she had always wanted to have kids; thinking having a family would cement the bond of their marriage. Charles was always too busy to discuss the possibility of starting a family and insisted that she stay on contraceptives. He said he just wasn't quite ready to take on the responsibilities that having kids would bring on, and kept putting it off, and so it never happened. Emma wasn't the type to go against his wishes, although many times through the years she thought she should have just gotten pregnant and had it over with. However, it just seems they both kept very busy with work and before she knew it, the years had passed, as did the opportunity.

No need to wonder about kids now, thinks Emma, as she runs on into the evening darkness deep in her thoughts when suddenly…

Chapter Six

Emma's daydreaming comes to an abrupt end and she is shaken back into reality when out of nowhere, she sees the flash of headlights and hears an engine roar. She realizes in a nanosecond that a car is hurdling through the air towards her. Being the healthy athlete that she is, her survival instincts shift into high gear, and she takes a nosedive over a hedge that is bordering wrought iron fencing. She lands in Vito's Italian Restaurant patio onto the laps of several startled diners. Diners who were enjoying a lovely evening were nearly frozen in fright but instantly realizing they too needed to scramble to their feet and rush to safety. Emma slides off of a diner's lap and rolls onto the stones of the patio and hits her head hard, knocking her unconscious. She saw a flash and then nothing as diners scramble over and around her to escape the confusion.

People on the street stopped as pandemonium broke out and a commotion prevailed lavishly, accented with shouts and screams. A horrific scene of people flying here and there, twisted umbrellas, tipped tables and chairs, the sounds of plates and glasses breaking and shocked wide-eyed patrons exclaiming, "What the hell!"as they hustle and push farther back to get out of the way of the car that didn't seem like it was going to ever come to a halt.

Finally, the steaming, moaning steel monster comes to a rest, and after a few minutes customers started to settle down and gingerly came out from under the building's overhang, where they gazed at the awkwardly perched, dented and beat up, huge vintage Oldsmobile. It's oddly cocked headlights casting a beam on the old building's brick wall, spotlighting the gigantic faded white letters of "Vito's Italian Restaurant —come in enjoy and relax."

Steam rose through the grille and around the hood of the old beat up Oldsmobile monstrosity that rested upon scorched shrubs and wrought iron patio fencing. Though turning ever so slightly, a determined rear wheel continued to spin, and stirred the damp night air. On one round patio table, a front wheel sat centered on a plate of spaghetti, smashed a small loaf of Italian bread that had one bite missing, the remains of what once was a delightful dinner.

The shaken customers gathered in bewildering chatter. The air was filled with the faint aromas of pasta sauce, garlic bread laced with erroneous pungent smells of antifreeze, motor oil, gas fumes and just the hint of cigar smoke.

Chapter Seven

Before anyone is able to catch their breath and realize what has just happened, on the street side of the car, where the driver's door is crunched in, out of the window crawls a way overdue for a shave, middle-aged stocky cigar smoking, brute of a man. He grunts trying to squeeze out the driver side window, head hanging down, he wiggles, arms flailing about, butt stuck and twisting about until he falls a yardstick's length to the ground. With a quick look around, he gathers his cap and wastes no time scrambling to his feet. He managed to collect himself and escapes in a half running, half crawling fashion, meandering down the street leaving behind the horror, destruction, and the oddly perched hissing auto at the scene of the crime. He hurries as he hears, "Who's that?" and then sirens can be heard rounding the corner at the other end of the block behind him. He panics, he trips and stumbles and somehow never loses the grip of the cigar he clenches between his teeth. Although escaping in a very clumsy matter he finally makes his way around the corner and down the street into the dark of the night as rain begins to fall again.

****

Meanwhile, back at the scene of the crime, witnesses conjured up reports to give to the two detectives who have just arrived. It's amazing the various insights of details that are reported although one remained most popular for the people who did not want to get involved, "It was dark and his hat was pulled down low and we couldn't get a good look."

Detectives, Sam Long and Marvin Jones, had come upon the scene just as the ambulance arrived and began attending to the runner who was trying to hang on but slipped in and out of consciousness.

"He was a fat old man, with a cigar hanging out of his mouth," noted an obviously upset gray-haired woman with a quivering voice, spaghetti sauce on her upper lip and wine spilled on her white jacket.

"He needed a shave," noticed a man, who said he was a barber, "and a haircut. I would notice those things. I can't tell you what kind of clothes he wore, dark colored clothes, I think," he added.

"He wore a fishermen's hat," commented an elderly gentleman who wore a dark gray suit, straight from the cleaners he said, and now adorned with splats of white cream and red wine. "What about my suit?" A sympathetic waiter heard his plea and magically appeared with a bottle of seltzer water and a cloth napkin and tried to clean him up as best he could which seemed to calm the old man.

"He wore dark, loose fitting, big men's clothing." This report came from a slender woman who was rather neatly dressed. "He reminded me of my sloppy, ex-husband," she continued.

And that seemed to be about the best the frightened witnesses could recall for the detectives. It was plain to see that the detectives had their work cut out for them.

****

"Is she dead?" asked one silver-haired, stooped little old lady. She wore a red hat and purple dress splattered with tomato sauce and spaghetti hanging from her shoulder. She looks down and points to herself. "Look at my clothes! Who is going to pay for my clothes?" she demanded to know.

Another diner complains, "I didn't even get a chance to eat my dinner!"

"Well, there's some bread lying over there," suggested a staggering diner who had arrived early to take full advantage of happy hour prices and was more than a little tipsy.

The crowd was becoming anxious and wanting to move on with their plans for the evening, but the detectives wouldn't let them go until they all gave a statement.

****

In the hours that followed, police searched the neighborhood, but the driver of the old beat up vehicle could not be found. Upon further police investigation it was discovered that the vehicle tags were stolen and the VIN scratched through.

As detectives Marvin and Sam pressed on with their investigation and questioning of the witnesses more pertinent information began to come forward with some shocking details.

There were reports of the driver apparently not braking and the engine sounding as if he actually sped up right before impact, so he could make it over the shrubbery, like he was chasing someone or wanted to get to someone. Be it intuition or gut feeling, three out of four witnesses agreed that the whole scenario had a criminal feel to it, as if the guy actually tried to hit someone. So the detectives could only come to one conclusion and that was that the driver intentionally tried to hit someone who was dining at the restaurant or he tried to hit the runner who is now being strapped on a gurney and lifted into the ambulance.

Chapter Eight

The injured runner mumbles something, perhaps a name, but ambulance attendants could not understand what she was trying to say as they checked her vitals and reassured her everything would be okay. Emma appeared confused and began repeating the questions that attendants and police officer, Peg, were asking.

"What's your name?" Emma was looking up and asking the police officer.

"Well, my name is Peg. What's your name?" asked the officer.

"My name is Emma. You have pretty eyes. Your eyes are so blue! I love you." Emma mumbled and then passed out again.

Peg smiles at the attractive woman as she slips off the runner's shoe pouch to look inside for an emergency contact name to call. Peg was still smiling and thinking about the sweet "I love you." A woman can dream, can't she, even an on-duty police officer. Somehow being battered and bruised just made the runner all the more endearing.

"I'll enjoy watching over this one," Peg decided as an ambulance attendant rechecked Emma's vital signs. They suspect a mild concussion and alerted the hospital of the approximate arrival time and patient condition.

Paramedics checked over all the diners who complained of pain, cuts, scratches and bruises. Those with more severe complaints were sent to Urgent Care. Surprisingly Emma seemed to be the only one seriously injured enough to be transported to the hospital by ambulance. Luckily no one else at the scene needed more than first aid.

Chapter Nine

Rain continued to fall, and the streets were highlighted by the glare of blue and red emergency lights as the ambulance with siren blaring raced to the nearby trauma center. The trauma center has been alerted and made aware of Emma's vital signs and personnel stood waiting as the ambulance pulled up. Upon further examination emergency room attendants decided that she had a mild concussion, would monitor her progress for a bit, but that she probably would be released in a few hours.

At the hospital, through moans, Emma gave the doctors her name and asked for Alice.

"Who is Alice?" the emergency room attendant, impressed by the apparent fitness of a woman her age, asked. He finds and calls the emergency contact information in the injured runner's key pouch.

Alice arrives in minutes and finds Emma bandaged and sedated. A few stitches in her forehead, that the doctor promised would leave no scarring, a slight concussion, two fractured ribs, abrasions, and bruising but nothing more severe.

****

"You don't think that crazy man tried to hit me do you?" worried Emma.

"Well, maybe he didn't try to hit you," suggested Alice stroking Emma's hair and kissing her forehead.

"If he didn't try to hit me then why did he run?" wondered Emma.

"Good question," admits Alice. "Well, maybe he was trying to hit one of the diners at the restaurant. Maybe you were just in the wrong place at the wrong time." Alice could not come up with any other logical reason except, "Or maybe he was scared, or had prior trouble with the police?"

Happy that Emma was going to be okay, Alice takes Emma's face in her hands kissing her cheeks and forehead tenderly affectionately trying to console her.

"Anyway, whatever happened, I'm so glad you are all right you poor thing!" Alice says as she lightly hugs Emma, so as not to cause her any more pain.

"I'm just glad you're here!" Emma whispered. "They took X-rays and said I have a couple of fractured ribs. Must have happened when I took a nose dive onto that table," Emma whimpers as she raises her arms to demonstrate her heroic dive across tables and diners.

"Oh, don't do that!" softly, but sternly, ordered Alice as Emma tries to demonstrate the dive.

"Ouch!" To add insult to injury Emma reaches for a glass of water from a nearby cart.

"Let me get that for you," Alice demanded. "Jeez!"

"Sweetie, you better just take it easy," she says as she adds more water to her glass and makes sure the water pitcher is filled.

"I'm fine, all that is fine. I'm not going to be here long enough to drink that whole pitcher, honey," Emma informs Alice.

"Want another sip?" Alice asks as she holds the glass up to Emma's lips.

"No, not now, I'm ready to get out of here!" protested Emma.

"Well, hopefully we'll get a doctor's release soon and I'll get you home." Alice promised as Emma moans when she tries to get up.

Alice realizes Emma's good fortune. She is thankful Emma's injuries are considered not serious and that she will be okay.

"Thank god you are alright! You could have been killed!" Alice exclaimed almost silently praising the lord.

"Yeah good thing I just got my will up to date and in order!" Emma jokingly smiles. "You'd be set for life!" She says looking directly into Alice's eyes smiling.

Alice standing over Emma takes a moment looking back into Emma's eyes and as she realizes what Emma has just said.

"That is not funny, Emma! Seriously! You could have been killed by that nut!" As she thinks how dreadful the outcome could have actually been.

****

Emma had her will revised after her parents' deaths and her divorce from Charles, making Alice the sole beneficiary to everything Emma owned including the bookstore and the living space above the bookstore.

"Yeah, what was with that guy anyway?" wondered Alice thinking about the evening's events and how things could have easily turned out very differently.

"I don't know. It certainly wasn't a heart attack, because the police said he took off running down the street like a crazy man," exclaimed Emma.

"There's your answer, maybe he was crazy?" suggested Alice.

"Why did this have to happen? I have too much work to do to be laid up," protests Emma.

"Hey, I can take care of all the stuff at the bookstore, sweetheart," offered Alice.

"And Tammy and Marie are there. They'll be glad to pull extra duty for you. They love you, you know?" stated Alice with confidence.

"Yeah, but they are always having trouble at the register, for one reason or another, and I need to be there," protested Emma.

"Baby, I don't know what I would do with you!" whispered Alice with tears in her eyes.

"Yeah! Nothing like being in the wrong place at the wrong time," admitted Emma.

"Just rest Sweetheart and try not to think about it," suggested Alice.

"I need to get to the store or at least check on it," Emma was already feeling better since the pain pills kicked in.

"I just spoke with Marie and Tammy. They were

so concerned when I told them what happened. They said not to worry about anything and just concentrate on getting better. They are so glad that you are doing as well as you are. You could have been killed you know."

"Yes, I know!" Emma acknowledged, but I'm still here.

Chapter Ten

Emma made the bookstore her top priority in honor of her parents' untimely deaths. Through the years, Emma was happy to see her parents mellow through marriage counseling. They had begun giving her more responsibility and themselves more free time. They got along much better as they aged and they had become more spiritual and even began to meditate and join yoga groups in place of going to church. They attended spiritual camps and workshops leaving Emma and Charles to manage bookstore while they were gone on trips. Their dream was to visit Peru one day.

Charles surprised her parents one day with access to a Siesta plane and pilot and offered to fly them to Peru to visit the ancient Incan city of Manchu Picchu. They were on their way to Lima from Cusco over the mountainous southeastern Peruvian interior, almost to their destination, when the plane crashed, and the pilot and Emma's parents were killed instantly. A hiker who reported the accident said he could hear the plane's engine sputter before it went down. It was such a tragedy just when her parents were happy and enjoying life.

It was amazing to Emma how her parents had changed through the years and how they had come to believe that we are spiritual beings living as humans beings here on earth. Her parents believed in reincarnation and that we may come to earth many lifetimes to learn to love one another. Emma's parents believed that all human beings are related to a higher light source; that we are all gods, a spec of light, if you will. Since they began their spiritual quest, they often told her that they were ready to go, that they did not fear death. That death is an adventure, just as each lifetime spent here on earth is. And we come back for additional lifetimes only if we choose to. Emma thought that her parents' spiritual beliefs were refreshing and agreed that we are all part of a light source. We should love one another for we are all connected.

Charles, on the other hand, thought that they were all losing their minds. But was glad that her parents were at peace and believed that they would reunite in the afterlife.

Chapter Eleven

Detectives, Sam Long and Marvin Jones, tried to piece together what just happened as they looked over their notes they took from several witnesses. The witnesses didn't offer much information on the driver who ran off from the wretched car. The only things they could come up with were that he looked sloppy, heavyset, smoked cigars and wore a fisherman's hat.

"It all looks suspicious to me though, Marvin," Sam decided.

As the police wrecker pulled up, the two detectives were looking into the car after they checked out the license plates and found that the plates were stolen from another vehicle. They checked out the Vehicle Identification Number but could not read it because it had deep scratches through it.

"Very suspicious! This was no accident!" Marvin had to agree with Sam. "I think the guy was out to get either someone sitting here on the patio or that runner.

"Something is very suspicious I think, Marvin." Sam

was becoming even more convinced when he checked under the front seats and found a gun. They slipped it into a bag and had an officer take it to the lab to have it checked for prints. The key was still in the ignition and the motor still running when the wrecker pulled up. Steam was pouring out from around the hood, and front grille and oil was dripping onto the hot manifold. Marvin instructed the wrecker driver to turn the car off and hurry and get it towed away before the car or the shrubbery caught on fire.

"Well, we'll see what turns up!" Marvin said rather hopelessly thinking that they didn't have much to go on.

"Question is, was this a freak accident, or did this man mean to hit the runner or one of the people who were dining on the patio?" Sam added.

"Let's go over all the information on the diners and other witnesses and see what comes up. Let's find out if the restaurant takes reservations and if they do, who was on the list and if they showed up for their reservation. Find out if anyone had a regular table on the patio where they sat all the time."

It was plain to see Marvin and Sam had their work cut out for them.

Chapter Twelve

In her apartment above the bookstore, Emma is resting and glad to be home. Alice helped her up the steps and into the bedroom. The pain pills were kicking in now, and she was getting sleepy.

"I'll call for extra help in the store tomorrow so you can stay home and rest," suggested Alice. Although she was half-asleep, Emma, was alert enough to protest Alice's suggestion.

"Oh, I'll be fine!"

"You sure you don't want to spend the day tomorrow on the couch or on the lounge chair on the patio in the sun? Tomorrow is supposed to be a beautiful day. It would be a good day just to spend the day at home."

"That couch is as uncomfortable as hell. I'd rather be on my feet and busy," mumbled a cranky Emma.

Emma did love her beautiful and relaxing home. She and Alice loved the spaciousness and open floor plan. They had it decorated with various art pieces and luscious green plants. They both loved the exposed brick walls and rich dark wide plank oak floors. But Emma was restless and wanted to get back to her regular work routine and keep her mind busy and not think about the whole ordeal and the absurd possibility that some crazy guy was out to get her.

"Are you sure . . ."Alice about to protest is cut off short.

"Oh no, I'll be going to the store tomorrow," protested Emma. "I'm feeling better since I left the hospital!" as she lay down on the bed and fell asleep.

****

Emma's bookstore is her life. She was there every free moment when her parents ran it, learning the trade and assigning book reviews and purchases, interviewing authors and scheduling book signings. The bookstore did well through the years and Emma wanting to honor her parents, treasured the challenges and the responsibility to uphold the store's sound business practices and reputation. Emma realized that business was good at the store and always had been because of their dedicated customers, some of which are neighboring business people and old friends of her parents. Emma's parents always reminded her that they had the most popular and best business location in town.

The streets there are lined with old oak trees, brick sidewalks and antique lampposts surrounded by tiny shops and outside restaurants and numerous coffee houses, specialty shops and antique stores.

For years, a corporation owning several bookstores

wanted to buy her out, and Emma refused to entertain the thought. She was adamant and insisted that the place was not for sale even though the price was substantial, money wasn't everything to her.

Alice worked at her own consultant business but helped out in the store from time to time while visiting Emma at the store through lunch, she helped on the weekends if Emma worked or while waiting for her to close up in the evening. They both just felt it was better not to be together twenty-four hours of the day. Alice had worked for a large firm and recently struck out on her own and was working to build her clientele. It worked out just fine having her office several doors down from the bookstore. In fact that is how they met, well, met again.

Chapter Thirteen

Emma and Alice had reconnected again by chance shortly after her parents died in the plane crash and she had divorced Charles for emotional and mental cruelty after she discovered his unethical business practices. Over time, much to her disappointment, Emma had come to find out that there was merit to her many suspicions regarding Charles. He had a tendency to enter into risky financial ventures, putting the bookstore at financial risk. He, having been the store accountant, was intelligent but slightly shifty, so Emma had discovered on more than one occasion. She often found mistakes in the bookkeeping. At first she thought they were mere oversights, but then she began to wonder why the accounting records were not balancing. The more Emma double-checked his accounting work, and brought it to his attention, the more defensive he became. At times, he became mentally and emotional abusive towards her, sometimes embarrassing her in front of Marie and

Tammy and even in front of customers. It seemed the family-owned store was not making enough money fast enough to match Charles's targeted monetary goals and he was becoming restless. After many conversations with Marie and Tammy, Emma decided to file for divorce. Marie and Tammy advised against it saying they thought it was a phase and that Charles' problems would work themselves out. But Emma was adamant, fed up, and filed for divorce. Charles was angry at the outcome. He realized that the store was entrusted to Emma, and that he would not get half from a court appointed decision that would have forced the sale of the bookstore. He took her back to court several times but evidently gave up and just went away; but he went away angry and vowed he'll get his just dues.

****

Charles was a sad and angry man and his marriage was unhappy because of his upbringing, so he claimed. If anyone had asked Charles, he would have said that he was only a product of his father's demands and expectations. His father compared Charles to his older brother, Joe, his whole life, through childhood and into adulthood. Charles could never measure up to the expectations established by his older perfect chip-off-the-old-block brother.

"Why can't you be more like Joe? Now he has his shit together," his father would angrily scold and shame him.

His dad would brag about all of Joe's wonderful accomplishments. Joe even looked just like his dad who was tall, rugged, and muscular with movie star looks. Charles tried working out at the gym every day for a while but was just not able to toughen up.

Joe received scholarships to all of the best universities finally settling on Harvard. His dad was quite proud. All would have been all right if only Charles' dad wouldn't have rubbed his nose in it. His brother was so much brighter and did so well in school. It seemed everything came easy to Joe. And so, all his life, Charles was always trying to win his dad's approval. So what if his real estate deals were a little shady, he got the land sold and made good money in the process. His friend, Bob was his partner in crime, so to speak. Ever since their college days, they did everything together both sharing the same unethical business principles and techniques.

Chapter Fourteen

The accident happened only blocks from the bookstore, so word had traveled fast to Marie and Tammy working in the store. Alice called them with an update on Emma as they were about to call her. Emma knew that Marie and Tammy were faithful devoted employees and would do anything for her. What Emma didn't know is that they weren't real crazy about Alice, for some reason they preferred that Emma be with Charles. They kept those thoughts to themselves; however, not wanting to jeopardize their work relationship with Emma.

****

It's almost closing time and into the store comes Penny who runs the smoothie shop next door.

"My god how is she?" Penny asked. "Is there anything I can do?"

Since the accident, the bookstore was filled with

neighbors and other regular customers wanting to find out what happened and see how Emma was feeling. The dining area and coffee counter and tables were filled with inquisitive and concerned customers and friends after hearing what happened. Tammy and Marie had their hands full but were so thrilled to see that people were concerned and wanted to check on Emma's progress.

Tammy gave Penny a full report and adds, "We're hoping she recovers quickly."

"Oh crap even the conspiracy monarch is here," whispered Tammy. And yes Georgette and her posse were there conspiring as usual and of course, each had their own theory about the "accident."

"He wanted to kill someone that was dining there at that restaurant and Emma was in the wrong place at the wrong time, it's in the cards, the Tarot cards," says Georgette. Georgette confides in Tarot cards on a daily basis and does readings for people on request in her self-claimed little corner of the store. Anyone interested in a reading knew where to find her in the corner behind the big plant sitting at her little round table with her deck of Tarot cards.

Edie, a member of Georgette's conspiracy group, little, bent and thin, with a hearing loss and who refuses to wear her hearing aid, loudly contributed, so she could hear herself over what was becoming a deafening crowd. "There's something fishy about all of this!" she proclaims.

"Yeah, there's something fishy about this all right, I can feel it!" Georgette agreed as she laid out her Tarot cards.

Georgette relied on the Tarot cards, the planets, the stars, her intuition and ESP to guide her interpretation of her constant suspicions. Georgette believed in the existence of secret societies, and reported daily on secret groups, which she said were located in places all over the world and how they hypnotized listeners with privately owned manipulated news spewed out on low frequencies. Georgette even thinks that secret groups manipulate the weather.

Then, Georgette steps in front of the crowd to say, "There are the full evenings' worth of brainwashing, commercials, pushing the sale of chemically infused foods, and drugs to cure those illnesses they say you have. The air is polluted, and water is wasted and polluted with all the fracturing search for natural gas that goes on and it doesn't matter because we're all doomed anyway, with global warming and all."

"Someone might as well make some money; I guess, we certainly do not. Rather, we seniors get more and more of our so-called "entitlements" taken away year after year. I resent that because I paid into those so-called entitlements for forty years and now big corporate heads end up with everything. And that makes me angry."

Since no one interrupts her, Georgette continues her tirade, "Yes, we sell books about it all in the store here. Just ask me and I will give you the list of some great conspiracy books." Georgette plugged the bookstore, then moved on to another topic. She is on a roll!

"On another note: Ever since the mid-nineties," she continues, "people all over the Southwest have seen this wonderful mile-wide alien craft. It floats silently with amber lights aligned in a V formation; with anywhere from five to six luminous lights that are self-containing amber beams. People who have witnessed the spacecraft are not afraid of it, but rather are amazed by it and feel a sense of peace and a connection to it. People who have witnessed it believe that it is a friendly spacecraft from another galaxy perhaps here to help us or show their might if we don't decide to straighten up and fly right. Reports have been made that spacecrafts have been seen close to the earth during times of major war events. Some conspiracy theorists believe that aliens are here to protect this planet, want leaders to stop invading and taking over other countries for power and monetary gain."

But Georgette had her own theory; she didn't believe that the spacecraft was filled with aliens she believed that it was filled with big shot corporate heads showing off their billion-dollar toy. Which would soon take the very rich to a space station near Mars.

When asked, or not, Georgette, will tell anyone, "Yes, that is what I personally believe, that this spacecraft is filled with humans who created and built it in collective collaboration by super rich, wealthy and powerful in preparation to escape Earth if any solar, cosmic, or lunar catastrophe that may come. I know, I know, no one wants to believe this, but can't you see the temptation of it for the super rich? The power to save themselves by living in space on a space station until someday, they can go back to Mars," Georgette asks and without waiting for an answer goes on. "Yes, go back to Mars, where they came from in the first place; where they lived until their greed destroyed that planet, and then they were forced to come to Earth to survive. Yes, their greed that wrecked their planet Mars, forced them to come here. And now look at what they are doing to this planet? Yes, there was once life on Mars."

"Just where does she get this stuff?" Marie whispers to Tammy in total amazement. "And look at the people all sitting there, mesmerized, and listening to her? I'm totally amazed."

"We have to stop ordering those conspiracy books for her, Tammy!" swore Marie.

"What? But look at the business, it's more entertaining than going to the movies, or a comedy club," laughs Tammy. "Make a note! I think we should order more conspiracy books." And they both laugh.

****

The place got so busy that Marie and Tammy wanted to lock the doors when they saw Georgette walking towards the store. She walked determinedly, with reference books in hand, and research completed and ready to share her findings with anyone willing to listen. She always had material and a reference to back up her statements and referenced books that were for sale and available, stocked on the bookstore shelves.

This was Georgette's new life passion now since she was retired and her husband passed away several years before. She came in and read all the conspiracy books. So Marie and Tammy got an ear full every day especially in the morning. It seems Georgette never missed a morning to come in and give a full report of her "conclusions" as she drank her coffee and ate her pastry, sitting tucked in her corner. Tammy would joke and say that Georgette was like a spy hiding in the bushes; head bowed appearing to be in deep concentration reading but also listening to nearby conversations.

"Those aren't regular hearing aids but rather some sort of supersonic listening device that Georgette uses," claimed Tammy. And she wasn't joking.

Marie and Tammy would tell Georgette that she was drinking regular coffee with caffeine when instead they served her decaf after they realized decaf slightly, but only slightly, toned her down a bit.

Georgette might be a nuisance but Marie and Tammy began to notice that Georgette brought in more and more customers. Yes, there were noticeably more customers, some giving their opinions too about things like the reasons for wars, the economy, global warming, the high price of gas and so much more. And they bought drinks, food and lots of books.

Of course, they all had their conspiracy theories regarding the car jumping the hedge and crashing into the restaurant patio.

And so it goes on at the bookstore and amazingly enough it drew a crowd of local residents and tourist alike. "It's better than talk radio or any conspiracy novel," a tourist commented to the television reporter toting a camera.

Chapter Fifteen

The next morning Emma was in pain, she told Alice, but only if she moved a certain way. In that way she got Alice's consent to leave the apartment and go to the bookstore. She was just unlocking the front door to the bookstore when detectives Marvin and Sam arrived, saying they had a few more questions for Emma.

"You fellows are up early," Emma said. The two men dressed in suits startled her until she recognized who they were.

"Hope you don't mind if we come in and ask you a few questions," Sam asked, opening his suit jacket and showing her his badge. The suit jacket was nice enough, just a little worn looking; it and the black butt of his revolver created a dull contrast with his dingy white, "ring around the collar" shirt. She thought that he certainly must be a single man.

"Well, I guess you have to do what you have to do," acknowledged Emma although she really didn't feel like being bothered. "Come on in."

"Well, we have been thinking that the incident did not appear to be an accident, so we were wondering if you have any known enemies?" Marvin asked pulling out a pen and note pad. He continued, "Maybe an ex that wants to get even, or an ex-business partner?"

"Well, I do have an ex and he was a business partner, too, so to speak." *How absurd, to ask these questions*, thinks Emma.

"What's his name?" Sam asked, poised to write.

"Charles Kingston," Emma answers reluctantly; still thinking this makes no sense. Her mind racing, mentally trying to tie Charles in somehow.

"Tell me about the divorce, was it amiable?" asked Marvin, eyes down, ready to jot down more notes.

"No, it was not amiable! He was abusive and he wanted the store which I inherited from my parents after they were killed in an airplane accident!" Emma's head hurt and she really didn't want to have to think about the ugly past regarding her ex or the horrible accident that robbed her of both of her parents.

"Look, I only came into the store for a few minutes and I'm not planning to stay here all day," explained Emma her head beginning to ache even more now.

"You live upstairs? Is that correct?" inquired Sam.

"Yes," replied Emma wondering why all these questions were so necessary.

"Well, who is Alice," asked Marvin still looking down at his notes resting his hand on his pouch of a belly. He absentmindedly pushed his glasses up on his nose with the other hand. His thinning hair, windblown, his brown suit wrinkled and jacket open exposing, stretched to the max, buttons that are ready to pop off his light blue shirt.

He sees where her eyes go, "Too many complimentary donuts," he readily admits. Marvin seems almost proud of his appearance, as the side effects of being a detective and sitting too long in his car on surveillance. One would think that Marvin didn't have a wife but he did and she worked as a secretary of the precinct. Neither Marvin nor his wife was much into eating healthy or exercising. They were a match made in heaven, Marvin often told Sam, who was only slightly neater in appearance, and stayed a little slimmer in an attempt to find a wife.

Sam was in his forties and still single. It seemed almost daily Marvin would offer consoling words such as, "Don't worry, for every pot there's a lid." This did not help Sam who was eager to meet someone and settle down. He wanted be married and be as content as Marvin seemed to be.

Sam had spent the last few years taking care of his aging mother. Yes, he admitted to being a mama's boy. His father had run off with another woman when he was a boy and it devastated him and his mother. He felt that he had to be the man of the house then and had to monetarily and morally support his mother who was chronically depressed. Yes, Sam dated through the years, but many of the women he dated grew tired of hearing about his mother, and they saw how he couldn't commit to plans and broke dates because of her. Sam, a detective for many years, worried what would happen to her if something happened to him.

Sam's dad was a police officer, and when he left the

family he moved to another precinct across town where his, much younger than he, girlfriend lived. It seemed to his mama that following in his daddy's footsteps as a police officer was Sam's one way of trying to connect to his daddy although it didn't seem to have worked. It seemed to Sam that his dad was trying to hang on to his youth, when he abandoned his mother for a younger woman.

****

"Alice is my partner!"announced Emma rather proudly, forgetting herself, and speaking before her conservative childhood upbringing mental tapes engaged and pride turned into feelings of wrongful shyness for actually saying it aloud. She was embarrassed now for answering the question the way she did.

"Business partner?" asked Sam sucking his gut in and standing taller wanting to make a good impression on the lady. His black suit was only a tad tidier than Marvin's.

"No! Partner, as in life partner!" she shot back, head bashfully lowered at first, and then raised with pride, meeting his gaze proudly. It was as if she was saying, "Don't give me any trouble regarding my personal life!"

"Oh!" said a more than slightly embarrassed Sam. And he turned red, slumped and relaxed his stomach. He was just thinking that Emma was very attractive and being single and all, he well, thought, well he could be interested; that is, after the case was solved. Being a strict professional, he couldn't mix business and pleasure.

Darn, she already had someone, But, respected the fact that a relationship is a relationship whether it be same sex or not!

"Well, how long have, uh, you two known each other, uh, been together, uh I mean!" states a slightly befuddled and disappointed Sam.

"For several years now," Emma replied. We met years ago but then lost track of each other and then one day by chance she happened by my bookstore."

Hmm, by chance? suspicious Sam wondered. To him everyone was a suspect until proven otherwise. Maybe that was another reason he wasn't married yet.

****

Happened into her store? That was putting it mildly. Emma remember it as if it were yesterday… she felt a sudden stirring just thinking about it:

Alice had come by the store while in the area on an exploratory trip to decide if she wanted to move her office to that part of town. Her plan was to start a consulting business. As she walked by the bookstore, she unexpectedly spotted Emma in the bookstore window straightening the book display. It was close to closing, and she thought the woman in the window looked familiar. Just then the woman looked up, and Alice's heart jumped. And yes, to her delight it was indeed Emma. She looked the same except her hair was almost pure white. She was strikingly beautiful. Their eyes met. Emma smiled thinking the woman looked familiar. It was difficult to make out who she was because of the light glare on the window, but she felt that there was just something familiar about this woman, and she just had to motion her to come in, meaning, "Yes, the store is still open."

It was magical! Emma realized the woman was Alice as soon as she entered the store. They reconnected in a moment with a warm embrace feeling the familiar warmth of past-shared intimacy. They reminisced of years passed. Emma invited her upstairs and brought out a bottle of her best wine, an old familiar favorite they both enjoyed. They sat on the couch legs curled under skirts just like old times. Emma invited Alice to stay for dinner and was thrilled, when Alice happily accepted.

After dinner, returning to the couch, opening another bottle of wine, they talked more with never a lull in the conversation until late into the evening. By the end of the second bottle of wine, they began flirting, moving closer and touching, and lo and behold they made love. It was magical as if all those years had never passed as if the last time were yesterday.

"Oh I forgot dessert," remembered Emma. They were sitting close, stimulated by the mood of soft candlelight and sweet music, and each other. They were giggling and flirting like old times, taking dessert to the couch.

"Chocolate pie and, oh, whip cream in a can," smiled Alice. "That brings back memories!" Emma was so glad she had just gone to market the day before, her intuition must have told her to because she doesn't normally buy desert, much less whip cream.

The kissing began and once again clothes came off, and whip crème placed in the most delectable places.

****

Rekindling the spark had come easy. They laid wrapped in each other arms, lying there trying to figure out why they ever parted ways.

"Oh, I think there was a guy involved, right?" Emma giggled mischievously. "Or two!" They had to smile on that one; why cry over the past and missed opportunities. What happened, happened, the past is the past.

"Oh yes," responded Alice. "The things we did. I am so glad society is changing." Neither Alice nor Emma wanted to delve on the painful past but rather think about a bright future.

It was love, again, at first sight. Emma had never really gotten over Alice she realized. A little more wine, a little more flirting, a little teasing, before you knew it… lots of kissing.

"What about you, Emma?" asked Alice. "I mean for the past several years who have you been seeing?"

"Oh, there were other women, the relationships didn't last," smiled Emma. Truth was, Emma stayed very busy with the bookstore. Oh, she dated women but no one seriously, seems Alice had always remained in Emma's heart..

****

Suddenly, as if to awaken from a sweet dream, Emma realized there were two men standing in front of her asking her questions and looking at her rather strangely.

"Ah Emma?" Marvin and Sam didn't know what to think.

"Oh! Oh, these dang pain pills!" she exclaimed when her mind returned to the present moment. She told the men the pills made her feel strange. Out of it! They'll think I should be committed! Who knows at this juncture in my life? She almost had to laugh out loud at the look on their faces. If only they knew where her thoughts had taken her.

"Shouldn't you be at home?" asked a concerned Marvin. "You look a bit out of it." He took her by the arm and moved her away from the busy cash register area and motioned her to sit onto a nice cushioned chair. "There, out of the way and nice and quiet."

Emma was beginning to feel embarrassed. "Oh I'm fine. Work is a distraction and keeps me busy," Emma said. Then she realized how nice it was to sit down. She felt better. The guys sat down on a nearby couch loosening their neckties and unbuttoning their collars because suddenly the room seemed to have gotten warm, or was it the telling look of Emma's blushing smile that made them warm.

****

They discussed the incident and the witnesses' comments and in conclusion as Marvin and Sam got up from the couch Marvin told Emma, "Well just as we did at the hospital, we'll have an officer stationed at your bookstore and in a car nearby to keep an eye on things for a few days in case this clown turns up again!"

"What?" Emma repeats, "If he turns up again? What are you talking about? You honestly think this guy was out to get me...for real? On purpose?" Emma just couldn't believe that someone was out to get her. Why? Who? None of this made any sense to her.

"Well Emma, you must admit," declared Marvin. "It does seem suspicious him crashing onto the restaurant patio and then running from the scene. Even witnesses say it looked suspicious. So, we are taking all precautions," announced Sam.

"But, why? I don't have any enemies!" Emma insisted.

"Do you know that for a fact?" probed Marvin.

"Are you sure there is nothing you want to tell us?" Sam asked.

"No, there's nothing... except a corporation wanting to buy me out and tear down my building and put in a big fancy bookstore."

Marvin looked up from his notes over his brown plastic frames at Emma and then at Sam. Sam meets his gaze and is matching his thoughts. He runs his fingers through his graying thick wavy hair and looks back at Marvin. They look at each other with raised eyebrows wondering if they heard what they thought they heard then both said at the same time. "Motive!" Standing there side by side, arms folded in front, with the look of confidence in their eyes.

"What?" Emma looked at one, than the other.

"Emma," that's called 'motive'," Marvin repeated.

"You two are something else!" She almost burst

out laughing. "You can't be serious!" She turned on her heel while bidding them good-bye and telling them she had to get to work.

Chapter Sixteen

After the "accident" and finally convincing himself that he was not being followed, Max circles back to the main street and waits at the bus stop to take a bus back home where he will wait to be contacted by his anonymous employer which he finds much to his dismay, doesn't take long. News travels fast in this area of town. His cell phone rings.

"So, Max how did it go?" asked the employer, as if he didn't know.

"Duh, I don't really know, I crashed the car into the restaurant patio, I think I hit her. Hit her hard… and had to get the hell out of there!"

"Well! You missed the target!" angrily shouted the employer.

"What?" Max slowly growls. Then, "Damn!" When the truth sank in, he knew at that moment that he was in deep trouble.

"So what are you going to do about that?" questioned the employer, his tone of voice demanding an immediate answer.

Damn, it seems everything Max tried to succeed in failed. He had a habit of showing up late at his big corporate security job; his immediate manager liked him and turned a blind eye. But when a fellow employee complained, his tardiness was reported to a higher manager, and his immediate boss got in trouble too for covering for him. But, then there were cut backs and he got laid off. He became depressed which led to drinking. He kept looking and tried other jobs. He was no good as a delivery truck driver. Well, his slight drinking problem seemed to get in the way of delivering beer to bars because he sat and drank at each bar; by the end of the day's deliveries he was soused.

He knew he had to stay away from the booze and the bars, so he tried driving a cab but then there was his hot-tempered road rage and the accidents, so he lost his chauffeur's license. Then through an unfortunate set of circumstances he became a hired gun. He owed gambling debts to a so-called buddy who said, "Pay up or do a job for me, or I'll kill you."

"Well, Max, you disappoint me! Just what am I going to do with you? And you call yourself a hit man. You certainly have a way of messing things up!"

"I hit her! She went down and I thought she was dead!" Max pleaded, "I know you have done me lots of favors in the past and I appreciate it, just give me another chance."

"Shut up! Give me one good reason why I shouldn't shut you up for good!"

"Well, you wanted me to make it look like an accident," Max complained.

"I'll give you an accident! Maybe you'll have one of your own!"

"But Boss!" Max was embarrassing himself by pleading and making his boss even madder!

"Now get back out there and finish the job and don't mess it up this time!"

"Okay, okay Boss. Thanks Boss. I'll take care of it! Boss."

"You better! Or you're dead!"

Chapter Seventeen

It had been several days and Sam and Marvin were still trying to get the pieces to fit. They had interviewed all of the restaurant attendees that were there on the night of the "accident."

"Sam, I see nothing here that makes me suspect any one of them may have enemies."

"Well, the one guy eating near the street named Dave admitted he was having an affair, and his wife just found out so that's cause in my book!" Sam pointed out.

"Hey, but the hit and run driver was a man!" said Marvin.

"Well, how about a hit man?" suggested Sam.

"Well, let's see if this individual named Dave went to the restaurant often and had a favorite table out on the patio."

"Yeah, we'll have to investigate further!" agreed Sam.

"Let's focus more on Emma right now. Who has something to gain if she dies?"

Marvin and Sam visited the County Records office and looked up recorded legal papers for Emma. Suddenly it became obvious to them. At the same time, they both said, "Alice? Why Alice though?"

"Alice is the sole beneficiary in Emma's will. In fact, she gets the bookstore and all if Emma dies," clarifies Marvin.

"Yeah but most people's loved ones aren't out to bump them off just because they are worth something. I mean Alice has her own consultant business and she's doing fine according to federal and state tax returns. So, why?" asked Sam.

"Come on, let's go talk to Emma," suggests Marvin

The two detectives are eager to get to Emma's bookstore before it opens for the day. Actually, both of them have an ulterior motive for getting there early. Without a word both know the other really wants to get to the Smoothie Shop early before the line gets too long. They have practically become addicts since they discovered the sweet shop on their first visit to the area.

They pull up and park the car and see the line forming inside the door already. "Come on, it's warm out this morning let's get a nice cold smoothie," suggests Sam eagerly. So the two detectives walk next door to the Smoothie Shop.

"Good morning," Penny's smoothie shop clerk calls out from behind the counter, greeting the two detectives as they enter the shop. They observe the line and see that they are not early enough. The line extends almost out of the door.

Fifteen minutes later, or so it seems, Marvin and

Sam finally get their turn up at the counter the clerk apologizes for the wait, and asks, "What can I get for you this morning?" Marvin and Sam see that Penny has at least three clerks working and that there is no more room for anyone else to work behind the counter of her small shop.

"Wow, you have quit a business here!" declared Marvin, to the clerk as he looks around at the crowded room. His eyes come to settle on the huge smoothie menu hanging high on the wall behind the counter. It takes a few seconds but he decides on a peach smoothie with whey protein with an added dose of lecithin.

"I'm trying to eat healthier!" Marvin claims, smiling. "You sure have a huge business here, every time we come by you have a line out the door."

"Yes, we would love to expand to next door if only that were possible. I know Penny has offered to buy Emma's bookstore several times, but Emma's not cutting loose. You know the saying, 'location, location, location' and this is a high traffic area, with tourists, and the courthouse near-by, filled with jurist, lawyers, and you name it!" reveals the clerk, as she works mixing their smoothies.

"This is getting interesting!" Sam says when he and Marvin step outside away from the crowd so more customers could file in. They were silent for a few minutes enjoying their huge and very tasty smoothies.

"Yeah interesting," repeated Marvin when he heard the remark. "Hmm, a motive?" he wonders aloud.

"I hope not! I'd hate to see this place close down! This smoothie is outstanding!" says Sam, as he stirs the smoothie with the straw. "Oh! Brain freeze!" grimaced Sam.

And Marvin laughs at the painful look on Sam's face as he holds the side of his head with one hand and the large smoothie in the other.

"Hey, I'm taking my time, I can't afford to freeze my brain. One of us has to figure out what's going on with this case." And he laughs again at Sam while looking next door to see if the bookstore is open yet.

"Yeah, I see Emma has the bookstore open now, let's ask her a few more questions," prompted Marvin.

****

Marvin and Sam have been visiting the bookstore in the past several days, several times during the day and noticed the huge crowd and certainly couldn't help overhearing all the conspiracy talk that goes on.

Sam offered, "What about that conspiracy group that hangs out in the bookstore, they look like a pretty weird bunch. What would they have to gain? Or they could be just crazy. Now that you mention it one of those guys is pretty scruffy looking like he never shaves. That Frank guy."

"I don't know. But let's check it out," agrees Marvin. "Let's ask Marie and Tammy and find out who some of these characters are."

"Who knows, maybe some are conservative Christians and don't believe in homosexuality. Yet, another motive," adds Sam.

"Hey, or a woman owning a bookstore," adds Marvin, trying to be sarcastic. Then, adding, "Man!" You're making this case even more complicated! You're killing me man!" They were both on sugar highs.

"Now we have Alice for greed, Penny, for extended property, the conspiracy book club members who possibly don't like homosexuality, and let's throw in just possibly a nut case," says Marvin.

"Or just a reckless driver. Let's not forget that!"

"Oh yeah, in a stolen car!"

"Well, maybe he just freaked and ran! It could be totally unrelated."

"Yeah you sure wouldn't hang around if your car was stolen–duh."

Just then Sam gets a call and it's the Captain saying that the owner of the restaurant, Vito, is having money problems because he is heavily in gambling debt to some shady characters who he is not naming out of fear. And, what's worse he was supposed to be sitting on the patio at a table eating with some investors, at his usual patio table near the sidewalk. And, get a load of this, right next to his table is a table usually reserved same time, same night by Dave, a realtor, married and cheating on his wife named Sue, with sexy Ginger.

"Jeez! This is getting more like a soap opera by the minute!" exclaimed Sam when he gets off the phone.

Chapter Eighteen

Meanwhile, in the bad part of town is another guy going, "Jeez!" as he tries his best to get another vehicle so he can finish the job he blundered.

"Jeez! I hate it here!" Max is in the worst part of town picking out another stolen car to steal, from another thief. Evil looking thugs are eyeing him up and down. There is no way he would dare come here at night! He spots a fairly decent SUV that is unlocked and hot-wires it but not before the two guys notice him and start yelling and shooting. Not a moment too late, he gets the SUV started but not before they blast away at the tires.

"Shit!" Max jumps out of the SUV yanks out his gun and begins firing back as he darts down the street and jumps on a bus rolling up to a bus stop. "That was too damn close." I have to think of another plan. Maybe I'll just sneak into her house while she is asleep and bump her off that way. The boss said, "Just do it!" Okay then I'll just do it.

Okay I must come up with a plan; think! The bus

ride is bumpy and the bus sways back and forth and from side to side and stops and goes and before you know it Max is fast asleep. He ends up staying on the bus until the Central Station final stop way across town where the driver is getting off duty and wakes him up. "Damn!" Max can't believe where he is.

Max gets off the bus and decides to walk back to clear his head. He demands his brain to think of a plan. He walks down the street and begins talking out loud to himself. "Okay, think! Break into her house. She, lives above the store. The store has an alarm system I'm sure. So that will never work! Keep thinking!"

Chapter Nineteen

Back at the bookstore Emma is chatting with the two detectives. "Oh come on guys, Alice doesn't have a mean bone in her body."

"We are not talking about Alice!"

"Who then?"

"We're talking about Penny!"

"Penny at the smoothie shop?" asked Emma amazed. "That's absurd!"

"Well, something fishy is going on and everyone else at the restaurant checks out; well not really," Sam, says under his breath.

"I'm not buying it!" says Emma. "You guys are reaching."

"What about these weird people that hang out in here; like that noisy, angry bunch over there!" suggests Sam.

"What about them?" asks Emma. "What? That's even more absurd! What the heck did Penny put in those smoothies, anyway? You guys are talking out of your heads," laughs Emma.

"Here's my theory," says Emma. Thinking she might as well add in her two cents worth, "I believe the guy that ran onto the restaurant patio had an accident, a simple accident with a stolen car, and who knows maybe he has a record a mile long and that's why he ran. Nothing more, nothing less!"

"Well, what Emma says does sound pretty reasonable, Sam," said Marvin, on the way out of the bookstore. They didn't even bother to question some of the members of the noisy conspiracy theory bunch already getting hyped up on caffeine and disgusting current economic events."

As they head out the door they hear Edie, who is near deaf, shouting, "It seems to me that big corporate business wants little businesses to go out of business so they can control the food that all the world eats."

And Sam says to Marvin, "Hmm, she makes good conspiracy point on that one, and a good business point."

Edie continues, "Do they really want all the fish to die so they can open up huge corporate fish farms? Yeah big fish, on steroids." Edie thinks she's got it all figured out, and there are some nods in agreement coming from the few people sitting around small tables, eating pastry and sipping coffee.

"Jesus, Edie, even you go too far sometimes," chimed in Georgette and a few others in their group.

"I bet that oil company could just crap for wasting all that oil they spill when they could be selling it," moaned the big guy in the group. He continued his thought, "Sure wish I had some of that money they wasted, so my son could get that kidney transplant he needs." And on and on, it goes.

"Sorry to hear that Frank!" said Georgette. "I wish there was something we all could do to help your son get that kidney transplant."

"Thanks, but without insurance . . ." Frank is so angry and feeling so helpless his sentence trails off and he just sits and stares into space as Georgette popped up with her opinions.

"That's another thing, these dang health insurance companies and drug companies ripping us off right and left," contributed Georgette.

"Well, Frank, I sure hope you hit the Lotto soon so your son can get that operation," consoles Georgette.

"That would be the only way my son could afford to get that operation," complained Frank, choking up. "These days you go into the hospital you never have any idea how much it is going to cost you—it could even ruin you. I know a woman who went to the hospital after she fell; doctors found she broke her nose and it costs her six thousand dollars. She had no idea."

"Where in the world can an average old guy make any money?" agreed Edie. "Where does your son live? Do you say in the Northeast? Hell all the drinking water is polluted with methane from those rock fracture gas drillings they are doing there. Not only there, I hear in at least in thirty-eight states. And there are those big tanks that have toxic fumes escaping from the top of them. None of us stand a chance," Edie said, almost out of breath. "We're all going to need new kidneys."

"You read too much!" someone hollered from across the room. "Now me, I don't want to know," said the nameless one.

Another customer popped up and said she saw on television where a woman, she thought she was a nurse, was tracking an area where she noticed a rare form of appendix cancer was reported. They suggested if you grew up or have lived for many years in that group of zip codes to have yourself checked out. The area was investigated and it was found that many years ago there were nuclear-waste barrels buried there.

"Yes," says the rough looking guy named Frank. "I can't afford to get a haircut and decent shave. It appears that there just isn't any work to be found." He goes on, "My poor son got laid off, seems his IT job in that big corporation was shipped to a foreign country. Says he had to train people from those countries and then after he had trained them, they turned around and laid him off! So no job, no insurance."

Frank said his son tried to get insurance on his own and the insurance companies won't insure him because he has something that they call a pre-existing condition.

"You believe that one?" Frank asked.

"Heck, yes!" shot back Georgette becoming more agitated. "I certainly do believe that one!"

"Seems it's getting worse and worse all over," Frank said, shaking his head.

"A new health care plan was supposed to take care of that and it doesn't look like it's going to take effect. And if it does the opposing group will probably get in to change and reverse it. All of Washington seems to work for the big corporations anyway, no one is there to represent us poor tax payers."

Georgette is still on her soapbox and the more agitated she becomes the faster and louder she talks and curious heads turn. "Why, my cousin Vinnie lost his job and the bank had to foreclose on his house. Then my other cousin, Vern got talked into one of those balloon refinancing deals and didn't realize it because they had him put down an exaggerated salary and after two years the balloon came due and he couldn't afford the increased monthly payments; now he's on the streets."

Sometimes a new customer will be so stirred by the discussion as to join in, "Well, if it were up to me, I would ditch the pro-business mentality of the government, end wars for profit and greed, global control, and control of resources. Wars are for profit for a few super-sized corporations that are favored, as in government contracts. I also would regulate banks and corporations. I would give lower tax incentives for jobs that stay here instead of going overseas, for home offices staying state side, for new developments of green energy. How about burning that high fructose corn syrup from genetically modified corn for fuel instead of oil? I recently saw a commercial wanting us to tell Congress we want to eat that corn and not burn it. Can you imagine that? Unbelievable!"

"Let's turn things around. How about lower tax incentives for small organic farmers raising healthy food in healthy soil and for raising healthy grass fed animals for food? If I ran the show, I would make decent health care available to every taxpayer and have our medical industry, drug companies and hospitals promote good health instead of a life on prescription drugs. How about promoting a life on healthy organic foods? What if you have a social (meaning taxes pay for healthcare) health care system that promotes good health instead of a lifetime on prescription medication? Our bodies are not made up of synthetic chemical drugs, our bodies are made up of amino acids, proteins, vitamins, minerals and elements of the earth and space; meteorites that have hit earth have been known to have more of these vital elements then the human body. Yes, we are connected with the universe. Our bodies are meant to heal themselves of illnesses and disease so why not take measures to build up the immune system with natural organic nutritious foods and allow the body to heal itself."

The customer suddenly realized she got carried away and the room had grown silent, then suddenly there was an enthusiastic burst of applause.

When the crowd stopped clapping, enthusiastically she went on, "This is what I want to happen," she continues. "A new consciousness unfolds throughout the world. I see now what is happening. We are experiencing a trend where children of today will not outlive their parents unless social consciousness changes to a healthier climate. But we will have to demand it. Vote on it with our dollars. Demand organic."

"Okay, now I am finished," the unnamed customer said as she grabbed her coffee, paid for her book and walked out the door hearing the room break into cheers behind her. Someone yelled for her to be sure and come back.

"I'll be back another day after I read this book; I
have to get to work, while I still have a job."

From that day forward, the open mic platform
became very popular as word spread and people
got a chance to blow off steam. It was the regular
customers who came up with an open microphone
platform where everyone gets up to ten minutes to
share their thoughts and make a reference to a book
that they bought from the bookstore. Of course, the
sales of many more books increased store profits much
to Emma's delight!

The forum got so popular and customers demanded
more food items so Emma had to hire more help. People
of all ages came to listen and speak their minds, buy
books, buy coffee, listen, eat breakfast, enjoy delicious
soups, sandwiches and desserts throughout the day.
Profits were up. The bookstore seemed to be a gold
mine and Emma was very thrilled with the customer
promoted open mic platform.

And it goes on and on like that all day, and most
days, in the bookstore. They read, eat and discuss and
find more hopeless, helpless stories one right after the
other but sometimes promising things too, like the
mentioning of the million or more companies heads
who are environmentally conscious and dream of a
greener planet.

They may disagree on many topics and sometimes
discussions become heated but one thing for sure, they
all feel that it helps to stay in tune and informed to

political and world events and respect each other's points of view. It's the protocol they all agree upon and adhere to.

Chapter Twenty

The bookstore may be noisy but in the apartment above it is quiet and the and the hustle and bustle and clamber of the open mic forum below is not heard by Emma and Alice who are having an intimate, romantic evening.

"Wow! Is it my birthday are something?" Emma asked. What a lovely dinner to come home to after a tough day at work and a rigorous run.

"I love you!" Emma moves in close and kisses Alice and holds her close as her hands begin to wander cupping her breast.

"You better stop that!" Alice mischievously smiles looking into Emma's eyes in an unconvincing attempt at protest. "Well for just a few minutes."

"Guess we better eat before we get hot and the steaks get cold." She says as she reluctantly removes Emma's hands from her breasts and leads her to the dining room table and uncovers the deliciously grilled steaks.

"Oh, and it's cooked just the way I like it!" Emma smiles as she slices into tender pink meat and takes a bite.

"For you my love, only the best!" says Alice.

"So what's the occasion?" she asks, then, seeing the bottle, "Oh, and my favorite wine." Emma smiles as she reaches for the iced wine bucket and pulls out the bottle.

"Oh, I just turned a great deal," smiles Alice. "So I am celebrating with my best gal—my only gal!" she corrects.

"Wonderful! Tell me all about it," wonders a delighted Emma.

"Well, it's nothing short of fantastic! I finally, landed a contract with a former client I've been trying to reconnect with for years. He's a big land developer," Alice smiled.

"Well, congratulations!" Emma smiled, as they clinked wine glasses. "Hmm! This asparagus is wonderful. Give me details on your deal; I'd like to hear about it."

"Oh, later my love, tonight is ours," smiles Alice as she leans over ever so slightly and kisses Emma warmly and longingly on the lips. "I just want to celebrate us."

"To our wonderful life together. Our happiness. Our success. I love you! Let's toast! Cheers to that!" Wine glasses clink and they tenderly kiss.

"Dinner was delicious. What's for dessert?" Emma jokingly breathes as she backs away a bit from the table comfortably stuffed.

"I have an idea. How about having our dessert in

the bedroom?" smiles Alice with a devilish wink as she holds Emma's face in her hands and kisses her lips.

"I like that idea," whispers Emma as she takes Alice's hand and leads her down the hallway into to their bedroom.

"Oh, I love this idea," Emma sighs as she slips out of her clothes with Alice helping and they roll onto the bed. Naked, smooth, silky breast pressing against silky breast lying intertwined in a state of sexual bliss. Never has a woman moved her as Alice does. She kisses her lips, her neck, and her nipples and moves her tongue down along Alice's beautiful smooth, lovely body. She can hardly contain herself as she becomes so aroused and wants her so badly. Her fingers and tongue find her and Alice squirms and moans with delight.

****

Later that same night, after all the love making and it's quiet and they lie naked soundly sleeping wrapped in each other's arms, neither woman hears a sound as Max comes and trips up the dark back porch and climbs the steps to the second floor apartment and manages to somehow jimmy the door lock and slips in. Trying to see in the dark he bumps into a few things that rattle and make thumping sounds. The hall tree loaded with coats almost goes over but Max manages to catch it before it goes crashing against the exposed brick wall, clunking his head. "Ouch!" he yelped all too loudly. Stumbling then collecting himself, he tries to tiptoe but the hardwood floors creak anyway under his weight. Bumping into a hall table, he opens a few drawers and pulls things out as if he's a burglar robbing the place or looking for something. The hardwood floors creak as he tiptoes in the hall. He's sloppy; he's dirty, and smells of stale cigars and booze; it's a wonder the stink doesn't wake up the two women, but they sleep on.

Max's career as a so called hit man never really got off the ground because he always had to drink for courage when he had to make a hit. Self-defeating, he needed a pint or two of whiskey to get his nerve up for this, like he did to get his nerve up to run Emma down with the car. Just like then, he's thinking that drinking booze first might have been a mistake, for now he getting all turned around in the dark and panic is setting in and he's losing his nerve and quickly decides to find his way back out of the building and call it a night.

Once out onto the back porch he manages to trip over the doormat and falls down the flight of steps. He feels like just lying there, but forces himself to get up, and staggers, then trips over a potted plant, then stumbles down the street; once again he fails.

Chapter Twenty-One

The next night Marvin and Sam are called back to Vito's Restaurant, seems there was a murder there.

"What? This is becoming a popular place—too popular," Sam points out, as he barely gets into the patrol car before Marvin hits the gas.

"Here we go again, back to the scene of the crime for yet another crime."

On the way there, the Captain calls and gives them more details. It seems that David was there with his girlfriend, Ginger, sitting at their favorite table and David's wife pulls up jumps out of her car runs up to the table and stabs David. When Marvin and Sam get to the scene of the crime, Peg the police officer, is aiding the ambulance attendant in strapping David onto a gurney.

"How is he?" asked Marvin.

"He's dead. Stabbed right through the heart," declared Peg.

"Man this patio is certainly becoming the scene of the

crimes isn't it? Speaking of which, how is the running victim, Emma? The one who owns the bookstore? I've been meaning to go in and check on her. There was just something about her. Like I felt I knew her in another life." She stopped, suddenly, she found herself embarrassed at the sudden outpouring of her heart. Maybe it was the result of this emergency situation, an adrenaline rush, this job can do it do you at times.

"I think Emma is doing fine," contributes Sam. "Uh, her partner Alice takes good care of her so I hear." Sam wanted to let his friend Peg know as easy as he could that Emma had a significant other.

"Oh, bummer! I mean I'm glad she's fine, I just didn't realize she had a partner, I guess," confessed Peg, lowering her voice as she started moving away with police tape to keep people away from the crime scene.

"Hey, go in and check on her anyway. Can't hurt," suggests Marvin. "In fact, we are thinking of stationing you at the door of the store for a while. Just in case. You never know it could be one of her loony conspiracy customers that's out to get her."

Marvin then winks at Sam because secretly they are really trying to fix Peg up with Emma and like Tammy and Marie they just don't have a warm fuzzy feeling about Alice.

"Weird, I know," said Peg. "But haven't you ever felt like you instantly just know someone? Like maybe you knew them before somewhere, or in another lifetime? Who knows? I guess when she looked at me and told me I had pretty eyes and she loved me; she was probably thinking of Alice. Oh well!" Peg sounded a little sad. "Got to go guys, hope I don't see you soon, well, not under these circumstances, anyway. I'll work the extra hours, if you want to station me in the store. No problem."

****

Peg was thrilled about the extra duty. She could guard the store and listen to the ten minutes of fame speakers whose reputations were expanding around the city. New customers came to the bookstore every day to experience open mic, which went on all day and evening. Peg had a few liberal, gregarious thoughts of her own. She just thought if only people were more aware of the collectiveness as a whole and got in tune with their spirituality they could work together for the greater good of mankind, instead of ravishing Mother Earth of her gifts. That came from the outward Peg side of Peg that people saw.

Peg's inner beliefs were in contrast because in reality, she was wrapped up in the game of greed of the mighty rich one percent who seemed to want to conquer and control everything. It was hard not to be caught up in big business these days. In fact, it was the only way to make a decent living. Even though big business was crushing the creative freedom of the small businessperson and leading more and more people into poverty and hopelessness. But, if you were caught up in big business, you stayed there, in its safety net for as long as possible.

As they walked away from the restaurant patio Marvin and Sam continued their conversation. "This is great, we position Peg to guard the store and she can get to know Emma better. Past lives? Reincarnation? Just don't know if I get all of that stuff?" Sam said, as they headed across the street to the car. Sam had a thought then and added, "I wonder if old Dave will reincarnate to yet love once again?"

"Well, if he does, he better hope his wife is still not out to get him," laughed Marvin.

"Hmm, I think Peg might fit right in with the to ten minutes of open mic folks at the store, then, with her talk of past lives and everything. Guess I'm just too conservative and old fashioned. I'm just an old married guy," says Marvin.

"Yeah, sometimes I even envy you," admitted Sam, feeling a little embarrassed exposing his softer side. A man has his pride, and it was hard to admit that he could be vulnerable and lonely.

"Hey, Sara has a cousin moving back into town; her name is Hanna." Marvin suggested as they strolled over to interview witnesses. Sam who usually did not consider match up suggestions agreed with the match up idea, especially after Marvin told him how nice Hanna was and pretty too. Detectives are used to taking risks he reasoned and looked forward to meeting her.

Chapter Twenty-Two

And so the days go on, in this historical, quiet little neighborhood with its busy sidewalks, shops, restaurants, condos, apartments, and tree lined sidewalks and streets of cobblestone. It's merely a pocket of spiritual beings striving and exploring here as humans. That is, if one believes in such things. Call it Karma, call it Destiny, we each have our own beliefs. Some people think open relationships are cool, some people commit murder if they hear their spouse is cheating. Dave's girlfriend, Ginger, ran off screaming and crying, never to be seen again. And Dave's wife, Sue, was handcuffed and helped into a patrol car and taken downtown. Her fate sealed. Well, unless she gets a great defense attorney who specializes in insanity plea cases. She could very well be out free in a matter of days as blatant as her husband and his girlfriend were as to have a regularly reserved table on the patio near the street for everyone to see their open love affair. Maybe it was Dave's wife who hired the hit man and he missed his target? Marvin and Sam questioned Sue and she denied the fact.

"Why, just tell me why, I would give someone else the thrill of killing the bastard?" asks Sue, in a rather matter of fact fashion.

"Well, she has a point there," admits Marvin. Sam had to agree. They both believed her. Who knows if she is telling the truth or not about the hiring a hit man? Maybe she did hire the hit man and when he botched the job at the restaurant patio maybe, she figures typical male, I'll have to do the job myself. I mean you never really know what goes on in a scorned woman's mind. Certainly she is not thinking rationally, or is she?" And the beat of life goes on in this wonderful historical neighborhood. Well, except for cheating Dave.

Chapter Twenty-Three

"So, my love it seems as if maybe the culprit in the attempted hit and run attempt got caught. It's in this morning's papers. Emma?" called Alice. "Where are you my love?"

Emma had slipped out of bed to the kitchen to make coffee and gather pastry for their breakfast in bed.

"What sweetie?" Emma asked as she glides in barefooted with tray of coffee and pastries.

"Oh, honey, that is so sweet of you." Alice reaches up to kiss Emma.

So they spend another hour or two in bed, chatting, sipping coffee, snacking on pastry and making love.

"Oh darn! Sweetie, what time is it? I forgot I had an appointment with Bob." Alice really didn't mean to say his name. Dang it slipped! "This morning regarding a business deal, I mean, appointment," she mumbles.

"Bob, your ex?" Emma asked, looking surprised and disappointed.

"The truth is Bob is stalling on the divorce papers,

and has offered me a part-time position in his firm while mine gets off the ground. I've probably mentioned it before. I figure I can work part time there. And the days I have no clients I can help you in the store as well. I would really like to break free of this guy but for now I need to stick around him until he signs those papers. I can't force him to sign them! I have no idea why he doesn't want to move on," complains Alice. It is plain to see that she is upset.

"No, I don't believe I recall you saying anything about working directly with him. I probably would have remembered if you had said something. I'm okay with it as it is, I guess." Emma admits to herself there isn't really anything she can do about it.

"I can assure you it's just like Bob, to drag this sort of thing out. It's a pain. But, I feel hopeful, if I befriend him. He wants to be friends. Don't ask me why! Well, not important, please don't worry, you have enough worry on your own without listening to my problems," assures Alice as she kisses Emma's lips, ever so tenderly. Emma wants to pull her back down into bed and stay there for the rest of the day.

"Love you."

"Love you back."

And Alice went off to take a shower and get ready for her appointment. By the time she had come out, Emma who wanted to go for a run, had to respond to a call from Tammy, in the bookstore, where the cash registers had locked up again. She'd have to run another time.

Chapter Twenty-Four

Tammy and Marie had always seemed very likable but a bit of an odd sort to Emma. It was nothing Emma could put her finger on, just a gut feeling she had about them. She met them in the store one day while they were listening to Georgette rant and rave. It was just about the time Emma had lost two employees and was quite busy. Tammy and Marie began to help out. They both said they had retail clerk experience and had just gotten laid off from their old jobs. Talk about timing. So, she hired them on the spot. Tammy and Marie proved to be good employees. Emma wondered if they were closeted lesbians, but the subject never really came up, so Emma continued to wonder, not wanting to take the chance of possibly offending them. As their employer she had to be careful what she asked. They lived close to each other, but not together. They dressed alike, wearing skirts and blouses most of the time; even their tightly curled locks were identical, as were their black and white zebra framed glasses. You never know.

Although, as much as Emma tried, she just could not get to the root of the matter. It seemed to her that Tammy and Marie were hiding something. They both were very religious and openly expressed their anti-gay opinions espoused from their Catholic roots.

****

Emma became so busy in the store that she didn't give Alice's mention of Bob a second thought. The store was bursting at the seams with shoppers, cafe dwellers and yes, Georgette and Eddie groupers. Open Mic Ten Minutes of Fame was indeed catching on. Everyone wanted to get up and state his or her opinions. It was quite something and truly a learning experience for many, to get a chance to hear both sides of political aisle, and the personal tragedies of the economic bust. There were many discussions of the W Bush eight years in office. One speaker thought the whole of the eight years were genius. This got a huge booing response from the others in the room.

"No, no, I don't mean that I agree," said the nameless speaker, "but think back. First of all, the Republicans do everything in their power, at tax payer expense, I might add, of defacing President Clinton with White Water scandals and to top it off for the clincher here comes Monica. So no one trusts Slick Willy, right? The media, the planted republican's loud mouths, and set the stage for a suspicious and sloppy W win. Remember Florida the ticket recount that goes on until February? Eight months later here comes 9-11 and then Shock and Awe. And I recall before that, certain politicians and businessmen wanting to get into Iraq and saying we need another Pearl Harbor to get in there and get Saddam Hussein. Now tell me people, weren't you ever suspicious of the perfectly placed video cameras that captured the planes hitting the towers? I mean perfect, no wobble of the camera; they certainly were not hand held. Makes me wonder actually when and why those cameras were installed." This certainly got everyone's attention and initiated small group discussion amongst the filled cafe tables. The room was abuzz with chatter and discussions as the speaker stepped off the platform.

Someone in the crowd added, "Surveillance, okay, I can go along with that. But I would still like to know when and who placed those cameras? Some sort of security company, maybe and why? Well, it certainly came in handy for on-the-spot news coverage, didn't it?"

People in the crowd are taking their ten minutes of fame and adding to what the previous speaker just said. The room was noisy and it was clear that the crowd was on a roll.

"Yes, and all this hype about weapons of mass destruction. Seems that was their method of entrance plan and they were going to stick with it. Repeat things, even known untruths, often enough and people begin to believe."

"You know, just a hand full of people own the media, is the way I hear it," contributes a guy, from across the room sitting on a stool at the coffee bar, sipping an espresso. The place was bursting at the seams. In fact, some bookshelves were moved to the far back near the restrooms to make more room for more tables and chairs. Every corner, nook and cranny was being used.

"Yes, and I heard textbooks were written that Saddam Hussein of Iraq was behind 9-11 when really I believe it was Osama bin Laden and his posse from Afghanistan."

"Oh who knows, anything anymore we only get what the media wants us to get, anyway."

Someone adds, "Funny how you don't hear much about Osama bin Laden anymore." And yet another adds, "You think with all the high technology we have surely they would have captured him by now?"

And so it goes. "I think they were looking for excuses to invade to get the oil. Yeah and sell those chemically engineered seeds all over the world."

"Seeds?"

"You know the one company that bought up most of the smaller seed companies."

"Oh, those seeds."

Georgette steps up to the mic and adds. "The way I see it, the big picture, is that there is a small group of ultra-rich elitists running the whole show behind the scenes and that their plan is eventually to have a single world government. I believe we need more women running governments because women care about the future of the planet so that there will be available resources for their children, while men in leadership positions are all about gaining power, and wealth for themselves. Men are more competitive while women will, in my opinion, work together for the greater good of mankind. Anyway those are my thoughts,"

Georgette says as she sums up her ten minutes of fame time, for now. Tomorrow will be another day and Georgette will have another point of view and that is for certain.

But what is so amazing about the open mic, is that there is so much that is said, so many different points of views, yet everyone participating is polite, sticks to time limit, takes turns and do not talk over each other, and when someone is speaking, the rest sit and listen until that person is finished, making their point. A customer commented one day, "Yeah, we are not like those talk shows where everyone talks at one time and you can't understand any of what they are saying."

****

Emma was blown away by the increased business. Not only were people coming in for the ten minutes of fame open mic, Emma had the step-up platform and microphone available for author's book readings and signings. With everything going on in the world, people needed a place to express their views, sound off, to regurgitate the news of the day, share the information they read in books and read aloud the poems, reviews and stories they wrote. Lights were dimmed, candles lit on tables. Emma purchased a special license to sell and serve a small selection of popular wines and beers. People loved the ambiance of her bookstore, the high dark ceilings, the exposed bricks walls; tall sturdy potted plants provided some privacy along the edges and position throughout the cafe area. On tables along the outer walls she had green desk lamps for reading and electrical outlets for electronics. Soft new age music surrounded the background; one could easily meditate if so desired. Emma began doing this to provide a calming effect on agitated speakers. It worked. The point got across but in a more subdued tone, more like a prayer, rather than a rant.

There was good energy in the room; Emma had a special area in the building where she sold, crystals, gemstones, candles, intense. Georgette and others did Tarot card and astrology readings.

Years ago, cars were built in this building; the wooden beams, paneling and food service counter were spruced up when Emma's parents bought the place long ago. Emma even restored the wood burning fireplace that matched the one in her large apartment above the bookstore. The bookstore was charming, warm, acoustics perfect for intimate conversation and that is what drew people in and caused them to linger. Customers were filling tables and buying drinks, food and books. Emma added more items to her menu offering more varieties of soups, sandwiches, and salads besides pastries. She also had a suggestion box and served what customers suggested they would like to have, such as a certain flavors of coffee, raw sugars, organic teas, and gluten free items. She made sure she bought organic meats and vegetables from local farmers, and vacant lot and roof top gardens. It all worked; sales were up. She even extended her hours to opening earlier in the morning and staying open later in the evenings. It's not just a bookstore; it's an extension of herself. The people who came regularly became friends and felt more like family visiting. It's Emma's pride and joy and she loves sharing it with friends and customers. This was her home surrounded by the loving energy of friends and books. She only wished she could allow dogs into the bookstore—she was still working on that one.

Chapter Twenty-Five

Emma finds herself wanting to be in the store more and listening to the ten minutes of fame open mic participants. One day as she listened, someone who appeared very familiar came in for the ten minutes of fame mic. At first she didn't recognize her—yet there was something about her. Her eyes were as blue as the sky. Miss pretty blue eyes took her ten minutes of fame at the mic. In the course of her ten-minute claim to fame the speaker mentioned she was a police officer, off duty at the moment, of course, she said. It was Peg, much to Emma's pleasant surprise.

Peg, the police officer spoke respectfully of the fallen at Ground Zero. She went on after her ten minutes were up but no one seemed to mind. So she spoke of the poor and crimes of the poor committed out of desperation. Seemed once people were down and out that it was near impossible for them to climb back up. She thought that there should be better oversight of the programs already in place and even more programs added to train the poor. She thought businesses should get tax incentives to hire the poor, to provide insurance and that the government should raise minimum wage. After all if people made decent livings they would be able to spend more money and that feeds the economy creating even more demands for goods and services. The room fell silent, which was truly unusual but she had everyone's attention. She continued on . . .

"You must admit in hindsight, looking back, it was genius. The whole eight years of that bicycling, cowboy's run appeared to me to be perfectly pre-planned all the way down to the bailouts. An inside job?"

"It was their way of managing and getting the most out of the growing housing bubble. Oh, they knew it was coming and that people with average salaries could not afford loans on those huge homes, nor the balloon loans that were strongly encouraged. The bubble had to burst sooner or later, so you might know you are heading for trouble if you have to be creative about refinancing and granting loans. Clue number one: Beware when you have people borrowing for the down payment too. And too many people were talked into refinancing and those fast talking lenders knew that those poor people would not be able to make the higher payments that would be coming up in the next few months. Financiers encouraged and said it would be okay to falsely state higher salaries than people were actually making."

"Actually, once again, it was genius — for 'them,' those loans were bundled up, and shipped off and sold to investors, many in other countries, so they were losers too. It was a way, in a way, to balance out the bubble of the housing market but at a loss to the consumer and a big win for the financiers. Banks ended up owning those homes and reselling them. So where's the justice? I can chase and catch the crook running down the street; sadly no one can bring to justice the crooks who robbed so many citizens of their future."

Peg stepped away from the mic and everyone applauded as she made her way to the coffee bar where Emma was standing, leaning against it, watching her. Her eyes glued as Peg strolls over to her, smiling as their eyes met.

"Hi," said Emma and she couldn't resist thinking aloud, "Do you come here often?" She wanted to laugh, she was giddy and her thoughts went on to ask, "What brings you to a place like this and I am so glad you decided to come on in."

"Hi, my name is Peg and you probably don't remember me."

"Hi,"replied Emma smiling and thinking, *Oh, I do remember you. I remember your eyes*, Emma thinks and blushes.

"I'm so glad to see you are doing so much better; are you?" asked Peg.

Emma found herself actually saying, "I am now." Damn, she didn't mean to say that.

Peg smiles a flirtatious, "I am now, too."

"You look wonderful," and Peg thinks that Emma really does look wonderfully rested.

"I'm back to running," admits Emma, almost feeling like she was bragging but was at a loss for words. That what was just came out, all of a sudden, she felt like a school kid with a crush.

"Oh that's great; when do you ever find time to run?" Peg asked looking around the busy store.

"Oh, usually mornings and evenings over to, and around the park. Running helps wake me up in the morning and after working long hours it relaxes me in the evenings."

"That's wonderful. I'm glad to hear that you are feeling well and back to your running routines," Peg smiles.

"I've heard so much about your place and the open mic forum from Marvin and Sam."

"Oh those guys!" says Emma jokingly. "They're here all the time. Actually, I think they come mostly for the smoothies that are sold next door."

"I just wanted to see how the one who told me she loved me, was doing," smiled Peg.

"I think I actually remember saying that.," Emma says, as she blushes.

"Well, here I am," smiles Peg with a twinkle in her eye.

"And I'm glad you are here," Emma smiles back flirting with Peg then Tammy catches her eye.

"Please stick around a bit. I'm needed at the register right now but I'll be back in a second."

****

And so it went on like this, every few days Peg would stop in, get coffee, sometimes speak at the mic, but mostly coming to see Emma. They laughed and talked about just anything and everything. It was obvious that a bond was forming. It was comfortable.

No rush. It was Karma. They just seemed to click somehow. And it seemed Peg was easier to talk to than Alice as of late.

****

Emma woke up as Alice slipped into bed, she might have been trying to be extra quiet as to not wake Emma up but it didn't work.

"There you are; I haven't seen you all week. You are always working it seems," says Emma as she scoots over so there is just enough room for Alice to slide in next to her.

Alice seemed distant somehow, aloof, as if her mind was somewhere else, preoccupied. Lately, their love making lacked spark and was less frequent as Alice spent more hours at the office and when asked why, just said she was working with clients but this morning she elaborated a little more on why.

"I have more clients, so more responsibilities taking up more of my time. I'm worried about keeping my clients happy and the business growing so I can pay my office rent," Alice says as she slides into bed next to Emma. Alice's words are muffled as Emma's kisses her. Well, Alice did want to sleep, but Emma was so nice and warm and felt so good she soon found herself aroused by Emma's kisses and smooth hand sliding ever so gentle down her body and then her soft lips caressing her nipples. Okay, the hell with sleep.

****

Alice knew that Emma was uncomfortable with the idea of her working with Bob, but Alice came home crabbing and complaining about him enough, that she wasn't really all that worried. Either she is really getting sick of the guy, are she is becoming a great actor Emma reasoned.

Emma often thought to herself and out loud to Alice, "I wish to god the man would sign those divorce papers. Why is he hanging on? I wish he would just meet someone and move on."

"I know, I know, Emma. He's a royal pain. He keeps insisting that you should sell your bookstore to him; that he would be the best one to sell to because he is willing to pay you a premium price. I keep telling him to give it up, that you are not interested in selling." Alice continues on, "The man is a nut case. He's like a bull dog with a bone. I wish he would just sign the divorce papers!"

"Tell him, sorry. I'm not selling." Emma is adamant.

****

Bob kept harping on Alice, "Alice, we need to get this deal finalized and soon."

"What are you talking about? She'll never part with that bookstore, so you might as well forget about ever buying it and just sell your client another location."

With that Bob rolled his eyes in disgust.

"You are the most stubborn man I know! Give it up Bob, she will never sell."

"Oh, don't be so sure," insisted Bob. "I have ways

of persuading people to see things my way," he boasted.

Alice had to almost laugh to herself. *Jeez this guy is stubborn.*

"Why not another location? This area is huge with lots of prime property. Why not another location and another business, maybe a restaurant?" Alice asked, but to no avail, her suggestions fell on deaf ears. Bob doesn't want to back down because he thinks Emma's property is the path of least resistance. He planned to approach her soon with a deal she couldn't resist and with details he adamantly would not divulge with Alice.

Chapter Twenty-Six

Max finds a note under his door, and so there are plans set in motion for him to meet his unknown employer in a secluded location. He is told to sit and wait on a particular bench in the park and to not turn around when approached by someone from behind.

It took Max a while to decide which bench, and finally he decided that he was seated near the correct naked lady statue. He finds the correct location, it's getting dark and quite frankly he feels a little creepy. He's a big shot hit man he reminds himself still he cannot help feeling a little nervous. Soon he hears footsteps approaching from behind him. His instincts tell him to turn around but he is stopped in time by almost muted disguised voice.

"Don't turn around!" A low muffled angry sounding voice ordered as Max begins to turn his head ever so slightly.

Max can't tell if it's a man or woman with a deep

voice, it sounds like the person standing behind him is wearing a mask.

"So, what are you doing about the situation? I have paid you in advance! I insist you carry out my orders or you will not like the consequences," insisted the angry voice.

"Okay, okay, I have a plan; a much better plan. This time it'll work, I promise. Here's how," Max panics when he feels the gun poking in the back of his neck.

"No! Stop! I told you no details. Just do it!" Max then heard footsteps turn and leave in the same direction they came.

As Max breathes a sigh of relief, he takes no chances and he continues to sit there on the bench a few more minutes listening to the tree frogs and owls conversing in a distance and hoping the footsteps do not return.

Chapter Twenty-Seven

"Good morning, sleepy head," Emma says sweetly and kisses Alice's head. "You got in late last night. Sorry I fell asleep, but I couldn't stay awake."

Alice looks up with sleepy eyes, smiles and looks at the clock. "You're up early." Alice is still sleepy but knows she needs to get up too. Morning coffee always wakes her up. She pulls on her robe and heads towards the kitchen.

"I'm heading out for a run before work," Emma energetically replies. "Call me later, okay?" She grabs her keys and is about to head out the door, her long silver, almost pure white, hair, shinning, in ponytail fashion pulled through the opening in the back of her cap. It looks like rain so she brings a light jacket to wear, over her tank top and running shorts.

Alice frowns sadly as she watches Emma. It seemed their time together was becoming less and less these days as both were kept so busy with their jobs.

"Aren't you going to run this evening like you

usually do?" asked Alice pouring from the timer set coffee maker. She loves this device, the aroma of fresh brewed coffee waking her up each morning.

"Oh, probably, I've been throwing in an extra run lately in the mornings. Just feeling chipper I guess!" explained Emma as she kisses Alice quickly on the lips then turns towards the door.

"I'm glad you're feeling better. Have a good run; I'll talk to you later, love," smiles Alice.

Alice stays sitting on the stool at the kitchen counter sipping her morning coffee thinking that in days past, Emma never would have gone by her just merely kissing her lightly as she was heading to the door. She stirs at the thoughts of Emma's full on the lips, lingering kisses as she passionately wrapped her arms around her and sliding her rob from her shoulders, caressing her skin, cupping her breasts and with her tongue . . . Alice was becoming aroused just thinking about it.

"Hey! Stop it," she said aloud to herself. Now she was alone in the much too quiet room. Sipping her coffee, she wonders what ever happened, to those days anyway. Why is intimacy and sex so difficult to communicate? Why are we always in such a hurry?

Emma shoots out the door wrapped up in her eagerness to get out there and run. She did feel a little guilty, and thought about the robe, Alice, her mind beginning to wander to her naked body underneath . . . promising to make it up to Alice.

****

The air was cool and crisp after a sunrise shower that

has since moved on, but leaving the flowers and leaves fresh and glistening. Birds were singing. The sky is a beautiful crystal clear blue, *Oh, much like Peg's blue eyes,* Emma thinks. *Could I be falling in love, no way, but maybe a crush? Now stop that!* Out of guilt she then pushed the thoughts of Peg out to the fringes of her mind only for them to creep back to the forefront again a few minutes later. "What is wrong with me?" she says out loud as she looks both ways before running, crossing streets on her way to the park.

But, for some reason, somehow it doesn't feel wrong caring for Peg. *Theirs is an innocent mutual admiration. Well so far! Now, Quit that!* In her mind, Emma, argues with herself. Can't believe I'm doing this.

But, never-the-less she continues thinking about Peg as she mindlessly darts across the street on her usual route to the park, to make one loop around and then head back home again, just like she does on her evening runs. Yes, totally disregarding safety suggestions from customers and staff at the bookstore telling her it is safer to change routes and the time of day that she runs. You never know when crazy potential attackers are lurking about. Tammy and Marie in particular protested against her runs in the park every day near dusk. Emma would tell them that there are so many walkers and runners in the park, that she didn't think that there was really anything to worry about.

****

Emma has been running each morning and evening for weeks now, same route. On this beautiful morning

Emma meets light traffic and heads to the park and gets on the paved park trail that takes her deep into the bushy and wooded areas. The birds are singing and she sees other runners and walkers enjoying the beautiful morning. There is a particularly lovely wooded park area where the path runs along a lovely rocky stream and waterfall. She loves to run through this area although it is a little darker there in the dense wooded area, but she loves the beauty of it. She rounds a curve and suddenly trips over something on the path and goes flying. Without time to react and try to catch herself, she's down on the ground. She lands on her side, down on her upper arm and shoulder and hits her head. Or did something, hit her on the head? Whatever it was, she is suddenly down on the ground and in so much pain that she feels herself passing out and lies there in an unconscious state.

"Bingo!" declares Max." Finally! Took freaking forever!" He laughs in relief. He finally did the deed. The thin nylon cord strung tightly across and six inches above the path worked.

"Yaw!" he chuckles aloud. He yanked the clear nylon cord from the tethered post and wraps the cord around his gloved hands with quick hand rotating motion, and in a flash, wraps the nylon cord around Emma's neck. She is moaning in pain. He pulls tight.

Emma is shocked, frightened, wondering what is going on and why is it happening. She tripped on something. Her head hurts, her throat burns, and she smelled liquor and cigars. She feels herself fading away again in shock as he pulls tighter and tighter. He's really angry now, this time he won't mess it up but she struggles and tries to get her hands between the cord and her throat, but then she subsides and stops struggling. Finally, his job is finished . . . with cigar still protruding from his mouth as ashes fall along with tobacco spit onto to her flushed damp with perspiration face, now still.

****

As if there truly is a god, suddenly, out of the blue and with the grace of an angel, a runner approaches from around the bend in the woods. He sees the attack and reacts quickly. The tall, strong runner begins to beat on Max's back and shoulders and smacks his head to ward him off. The attacker lets up but pushes the runner with his elbow. The runner comes back with more as Max rises up and kicks the runner in the knees with his heavy shoe before running off into the deep wooded area.

Max keeps running until he feels it is safe then, out of breath begins to walk like the other walkers who are also dressed in sweats and out for a brisk walk in the park. He easily blends in fully by the time he reaches the more populated area of the park.

The runner although in pain from the kick, tries to revive Emma. He sees that she is breathing ever so slightly. He jumps up and down yelling for help and finally attracts another runner who runs to find someone with a cell phone to call 911. In a few minutes, other walkers and runners are helping him flag down the emergency vehicle when it arrives. The attendants drive in as close as they can then run carrying a stretcher over to where Emma is lying. The runner talks gently to Emma asking her name, where she lives, just to keep her busy. They continue to try to keep her focused on the present so she doesn't slip back into unconsciousness again.

In the ambulance, Emma moans and speaks only above a whisper and asked. "Police . . . where is Peg? Police," then slips into unconsciousness.

The attending medic tries to comfort Emma and listens as she speaks but has a hard time figuring out what she is trying to say and determines she is speaking of Peg, a police officer. By the time the ambulance arrives at the hospital Peg, in uniform and on duty, is there. Seems in this part of town even being a fairly new officer, Peg is well known because of her friendliness and outgoing social manner of speaking to the public while patrolling the streets on the police bicycle or in the police cruiser.

"She's going to be alright," the attending medic updated Peg on all crucial vital sign indications and on what happened; that she was indeed attacked and a serious attempt was made on her life.

"Just what is going on with me?" asked Emma. "What is going on? Runners carry no money..."

"The man was out to kill you my dear. Did he try to rape you?" Peg tried to ask in the calmest way as to not further upset Emma. "Did he ask for money, search for money?" asked Peg.

"No. Maybe he had me mistaken for someone else," Emma mutters, still trying to make sense of it all.

Just then Alice comes running in the emergency

room. Medics in the ambulance had called the emergency contact number in Emma's runner's shoe punch.

"My gosh, what happened?" Alice was clearly alarmed and after taking a look and gasping at the gash on Emma's neck, cradled her in her arms and kissed her head.

"I never heard of an attacker appearing in broad daylight in the park!" cried Alice.

"Neither have I," Peg said, after introducing herself. "But I'm fairly new to the force."

Within an hour after talking to the female psychologist and trauma officer, and enduring yet another thorough physical exam, Emma was declared ready to be discharged along with prescriptions for anxiety and pain pills.

Before Emma was released, Marvin and Sam stopped by to speak with her.

After greetings were exchanged and Marvin and Sam asked how she was doing, Emma described the incident to them. Marvin couldn't resist asking her, "So, you still don't think someone is out to get you?"

Unless it was two separate incidences, Marvin and Sam were practically convinced that Sue, David's wife had hired a hit man to kill her husband. Did Sue not hire the guy as she said? Was the murdering of David a totally different situation? Was the hit man out to get Emma? The defectives were clearly confused but just maybe things were becoming clearer; that is, if this was the second attempt on Emma's life and it was beginning to appear that it might be.

"Okay let's think about this again. First of all, we

don't know who the guy was after in the other incident; we don't know if this guy is the same guy. So this could totally be a random situation. We are waiting for the DNA report on hair found in the car at the restaurant to see if anything matches any DNA if found on your neck or clothing," reports Marvin.

Marvin and Sam questioned Alice and Peg. Alice, with tears in her eyes, swears she knows of no one wanting to harm Emma.

"Well, you guys are the detectives, if you truly think that this was outright attempt on Emma's life then figure out why, before someone actually is successful," Alice pleads. "If someone is after Emma, then why are they after her?" demanded Alice. She was clearly shaken by this event and the earlier event that injured Emma.

"We don't know yet, but trust me, we will find out!" Marvin hoped that he was successful in making that sound like a threat to Alice as if they suspected her to be involved in the attempts on Emma's life and he could tell that Alice sensed his suspicions.

"The bookstore is a public place; anyone could just walk in and try an attempt on her life. We need to get to the bottom of this right away. This time was clearly no accident. It's a whole new ballgame now," declared Marvin.

"Unless the perpetrator picked the wrong victim, there are many runners in the park," suggested Peg.

"You would have to think of that," groaned Marvin. This case was getting complicated enough with so many possible motives.

Sitting up on the hospital bed, a shaken up but fiercely determined Emma holds onto Alice's hand as she helps her out of the bed after the doctor reluctantly released her. He warned that her she might still be in shock.

Chapter Twenty-Eight

"She's still alive!" shouted The voice on the phone yelling at Max.

"You messed up again." The voice said. "You clown. You are a dead man!"

Max shuddered as he heard the phone click. He stood there with the receiver in his hand shaking like a leaf. He knew he had to get out of town and fast. He threw a few things in a bag, checked his pockets to see how much cash he had and rushed out of the door and headed for the nearest bus station.

Unfortunately on his way to the bus station there was a terrible accident. A delivery truck hit Max. It seemed that Max must have tripped and fell in front of the truck just as the truck was racing to get through a yellow light. After the truck had struck him, it sped off. No witnesses came forward.

The dead man appeared poor and homeless, said the police. They could not find any identification in his possession, just a couple of notes in his pockets and a piece of clear nylon cord. Since it happened in their precinct, the chief notified Marvin and Sam and hearing about the notes and nylon cord they got right on it getting pathology and forensics involved. They were beginning to think there was no such thing as a coincidence or random accident.

Their suspicions were on target; Emma's blood and DNA were on the nylon cord. The notes of meeting places put the man somewhere near the park right before Emma's attack and near the scene of the crime at the restaurant although there were no dates on the notes, there were times and street routes written down that according to Emma was much like the route she always takes when she runs.

"Sweetie, didn't I ask you to never run the same route over and over?" Alice asked accusingly. "Like it's to be expected someone is going to attack you if they know your route and you run the same time most days. Perverts watch and wait for opportunities."

"But, this happened in the morning, and I usually run in the evening. And, after I was hurt at the restaurant, I didn't even run for a while," protested Emma. *Hmm, so did he know I was out there?* wondered Emma.

"Lately, though, you have been running both morning and evenings on a daily basis," interjects Alice. "And for long enough for someone to watch and wait for you."

Marvin and Sam received a call from the chief to check on evidence on another case so they bid farewell to the women and reassured Emma that police protection will be stationed at her bookstore. Emma didn't put up much of a protest but rather considered the guard at the door a good thing. Emma's change of heart led Marvin and Sam to think that she was indeed getting worried that she may be the target, after all.

****

After a few days, Emma was back at the store. Upon hearing this, the detectives, after getting a smoothie at Penny's went over to ask a few more questions. She appears slightly distracted and a little worried but still maintained her sense of humor.

She greeted the officers. "Should you really be eating that on duty?" Emma grinned.

"Aw, (slurp, slurp)," Sam was trying to finish his smoothie.

"Where's mine?" she jokingly asked. "Ouch." Her neck still hurt.

"Oh, we're so sorry. Marvin go back over there and get her one," demanded Sam.

"I'll have a large strawberry banana," ordered Emma, thinking a cold smoothie would feel really good for her throat.

"Thanks that's very sweet and I could use a treat," she responded when Marvin wouldn't take any money from her.

Sam began the questioning as Marvin headed out the door to get Emma a smoothie from Penny's.

"Sounds like this character was tipped off as to your whereabouts on that particular morning?" suggested Sam.

"Tipped off?" Emma was puzzled. Sam quickly

changed the subject. It's his own technique to throw people off guard.

"So, Emma, how are you and Alice getting along these days?" Sam asked.

Emma hesitates taken back at first by the question but then decides to answer it.

"Well, I think, umm, we are fine?" Emma was becoming confused and her head was beginning to hurt now.

"You are hesitating just a bit there, Emma," suggests Sam

"Well, actually I really haven't thought that much about it," Emma tells Sam but in her heart she thinks that Alice has seemed a little distant lately.

"Oh, she's just been very wrapped up in promoting a new client to her business." Emma's thinking was a hazy today due to the pain medicine the doctors prescribed for her.

"Why are you asking that anyway?" quizzed Emma. She was suddenly feeling tired and headed to a stool at the snack bar counter.

"Well, she stands to gain the most by your death," offered Sam, then thinking that he blurted that out louder than he had intended.

"That's preposterous," argued Emma. "I won't stand for that kind of talk. She loves me!" Emma insisted.

Sam thinks, "Well sometimes things do change, feelings do change." He didn't have the heart to suggest that to her though.

"Does she know she is full beneficiary of all your possessions, including the bookstore, its contents, and

the building, your apartment and its contents?" asked
Sam.

"I can't believe you are even suggesting . . ."

"We have been investigating some of Alice's
businesses practices. All public record, you know."

"What, you can't do that?" scolded Emma.

"We assure you it's all a matter of public record and
tax filings," explained Sam.

"But why would you even suspect Alice," asked
Emma. She grimaced in pain as the bandage on her
neck pulled when she turned her head to look at Sam.

"Well, we suspect you may be in some kind of
danger otherwise we wouldn't be checking things out."
Marvin suggested as he returned, handing her the fresh
strawberry banana smoothie which tasted so good and
felt soothingly cold as she sipped through the straw.

"Why would I be in danger?" asked Emma. "Why
would she even want all of this, she has her own
business?"

"It seems this property is in high demand by several
people and several business chains," explained Sam.
"I'm sure you have been approached."

"Why yes I have, but I can't believe people would
go to such great lengths to get their hands on this
property."

"Well that is what we are going to find out." Marvin
was determined to get to the bottom of this. "Come on
Sam, let's head back downtown and look through some
more records."

Emma, not feeling well at all at this point took
Sam and Marvin's advice and headed upstairs to her
apartment to lie down.

Chapter Twenty-Nine

So the next step was to find out just who was in Alice's will if she had one, that is. She did own a business. Marvin and Sam again peered into public records and found that a guy named Bob was her main benefactor of all her worldly possessions.

"Hmm, Bob," points out Marvin, "I don't think that Alice is actually divorced is she? If Alice inherits the bookstore and something happens to her, then by all rights Bob would get everything."

"We need to watch these two closely," suggested Sam.

"Right now, nothing really leads to them," suggests Sam. "Just this will and that's not a crime, nor is being married."

"Yeah, I know, that is why we have to keep a close watch on them," advises Marvin.

"What about Penny, she wants to buy the bookstore too; maybe she is trying to scare Emma into selling it," suggests Sam.

"This could really get sticky!" Marvin adds. "By the way, get the pun—sticky—as in smoothies, sticky?" No reaction from Sam, he's deep in thought. And actually ashamed that they stopped on the way downtown and got another smoothie—for lunch. "Okay then, forget it!" chuckles Marvin sheepishly.

"This is not funny anymore. My pants are tight and I feel miserable. What woman is going to want me?" protested Sam.

"Oh, Hanna loves you just as you are and you know it," smiles Marvin.

Finishing up at the records department Sam asked Marvin. "So, tell me what you think about this scenario. So, here's the story. Alice wants the store, it's the reason she rekindled with Emma after all these years. What an opportunity when she realized who owned the bookstore."

"You see, Alice got a grand deal of a suggestion from her husband, Bob, that if they acquired the bookstore they could sell it to one of the chains who have approached Alice in the bookstore while Emma was not there. She tells the big chain people that she would try to persuade Emma to sell."

"But little did Alice know that Bob has also struck a deal with Penny, the smoothie store operator, who was left millions by her late spouse and wants to expand her store and needs the bookstore space. Also little did Alice or Emma know that Peg's new husband Charles Kingston, yes, Emma's ex-husband, a self-proclaimed rich and successful commercial real estate broker and manager struck a deal with big corporate. Alice knows none of this but she does know that Emma won't sell."

"Either way, Bob's a winner, or is he? If Alice finds out, Bob is toast," notes Sam.

"Let's not tell Emma her ex is married to Peg," suggests Sam. "I truly do not think she knows that. I can't believe you thought to look that up. I'm as surprised as you are."

"Someone is trying to kill Emma, but who, is still the question," states Marvin.

"Of course Alice, still stands to gain it all even on her own without Bob, because Alice is sole inheritor in Emma's will. Of course this is just all conjecture at this point," concedes Marvin.

Sam goes on adding his two cents, "Alice thinks Bob is trying to kill Emma, and she is terribly frightened because if Bob is trying to kill Emma that means she is next because Bob is Alice's sole beneficiary in her will. She needs to get that will changed and fast and make sure he knows that she changed it. Of course he may just kill her out of spite then — who knows? Either way, so far all this is just speculation?"

"So who hired the hit man?" asked Marvin.

"My God man! My head is spinning," protests Sam.

"Come on man, you have to admit some of it makes sense and could easily play out," stresses Marvin.

Chapter Thirty

Emma rests while she waits for Alice to get home. She is thinking about Peg and the twists and turns her life has taken through the years and now even more recently. To be without love for so many years while with Charles and then comes Alice back into her life, and now she finds herself infatuated with Peg. What is that all about?

Emma, parents who were thrifty but not when it came to her education. Her parents sent her to the finest schools. She was popular, still popular she thinks as she looks in the bathroom mirror, as she gets ready for bed. Her father's first love was investing and he made fine investments in the stock market as he worked as a financial broker. Buying the bookstore was his second love for himself, and for her, and her mother. They loved books. They had skimped and saved and the finally one day decided they skimped and saved long enough. When their home bookstore property was paid off they began planning vacations. It was just too sad that when they finally got to a point where they could enjoy themselves and travel that they were killed in a plane crash.

****

Emma never knew that her father came by his money in some rather shady dealings. When she first married, Charles, he told her as much, but she didn't want to hear it. At the time Emma didn't want to believe it and choose not to. But she was sure Charles wasn't mistaken for he conducted a few business dealings with her father himself, of this she was sure. Emma was beginning to wonder if the plane crash in Peru was really an accident?

Lately Emma was not able to sleep well. Who could sleep after two possible attempts on their life? Too coincidental! These two incidents could not have been coincidental accidents. Her suspicions were giving her a queasy feeling in the pit of her stomach.

At this point Emma didn't know who to trust. Could it be the sedatives she was taking to help her sleep were making her paranoid? Were they making her even more paranoid then she already was?

What was she going to do? She was glad that Marvin and Sam kept security officers posted at the bookstore.

Emma was even more concerned and troubled to learn that the man who tried to kill her was then killed himself. She suspected his death was no accident. She thought it odd that the man who attempted to kill her was himself killed shortly after the attempt on her life. Why? Was he a rapist, a robber, just a nut case, or did he botch a job? A job where he was supposed to kill her?

This was all getting to be too crazy for her and she felt as if she was going to have a nervous breakdown. She wished it wasn't so late so she could go for a run. Running always seemed to help calm her anxiousness and well as give her time to think and work through what was ever bothering her. She wondered where Alice was? It was getting late and usually Alice was home by now. Where is she anyway she thought as she decided to take a Valium to ease her mind. Maybe I just need to sleep. So much has been happening lately. She drifts off to sleep and dreams about Peg's pretty blue eyes.

Chapter Thirty-One

The next morning, after a fairly restful night of sleep, Emma goes for a short run, showers and then heads down to the bookstore just in time to see Peg coming in for a quick visit.

"My, what a lovely early morning surprise and in uniform. Hot! Oh, no disrespect intended, officer, I assure you!" Emma smiles.

"What can I do for you officer?"

Peg just smiles; she needs to behave in a professional manner, for she is in uniform and on duty, after all.

"I just came for a quick visit to see how you are doing," says Peg.

"Oh, how sweet," Emma replies and continues, "How about a cup of coffee?" as she takes the "closed" sign out of the window. Peg follows her over to the counter, where Tammy and Marie have already begun preparing drinks and food for the day. The coffee was fresh and hot.

Positioned at the counter, Peg gets a bit of a chance to watch Emma work at the register, signing deliveries, and unpacking books. She makes sure there are enough coffee and food supplies in the inventory.

It seemed that every few minutes Emma is raising her head to smile at Peg.

Peg finishes her coffee, smiles, waves and mouths, "See you later" as she heads for the door to leave to go to work.

****

Marie wonders why she hasn't seen Alice come or go throughout the day, since she works right down the street. Even Tammy asked where Alice has been. "I'm just concerned about you Emma," admitted Tammy.

"Well, she got home late last evening I guess. I was already asleep with the help of a Valium. She was still sleeping when I went for my run and gone when I got back home to shower to come to work," professed Emma.

"I must admit, she seems distant or is it my imagination. I just don't know what I think any more," confessed Emma

"I know she is being kept busy with a big client. She left a sweet note, non-the-less. So that was good!"

At this point Emma is trying to make the situation sound better than what it is, and in so doing must admit to herself that things have changed somehow. She has had what is apparent now as two attempts on her life. Why? It is becoming obvious to her that she is the target and probably for her bookstore. The thought that

122

someone would commit murder to obtain a property extended way past her realm of imagination but she must bring herself to believe it. And now she even wondered about her parent's untimely, tragic death, and how someone had the audacity to approach her at the funeral and ask her to sell the bookstore. She was in such shock at the time she had forgotten that a business man had approached her as she was walking away from the grave site.

"Well, Emma, we have your back," said Marie "And if there is anything we can do to help you, please do not hesitate to ask." Marie and Tammy were a huge help to her, especially with all this other stuff going on. She certainly appreciated them.

Emma continues her work at the store, checking the books, working with her accountant in the back office, helping out at the register, greeting customers at the snack bar and café while listening to the Ten Minutes of Fame speakers.

****

Later in the day, Emma is busy chatting with a customer and doesn't notice Peg come back into the store to take her post at the door until she sees some customers look that way and whisper. She feels that they are a bit on edge and then sees why.

"Oh hi Peg, on your afternoon break?" asks Emma.

"Well, didn't Marvin or Sam tell you? I'm here on official business to be stationed at your door until further notice."

"You're kidding?" Emma was surprised.

"No, I'm not kidding!" smiles Peg.

"Well, it is wonderful to see you, but I prefer not on an official basis," complained Emma. "I'm afraid an officer stationed at the door will frighten my customers."

"Well, I realize that may be a concern to you and I'm sorry, it is out of my hands."

"I like seeing you but I wonder if you could you come in street clothes as to not alarm my customers?"

"Well, I suppose I could. Let me check with headquarters."

"So, what is going on?" Edie and Georgette and Frank are all grouped together now and wondering what is going on.

Emma feels she must be honest with them and explains that the two detectives, Marvin and Sam, felt the need to have a police officer's presence in the store. And that she has just requested the officer dress in street clothes while being stationed in the store to ward off alarm especially with all that has been going on. She asks her customers if they feel safer with the formal uniform or would they rather the officer be in plain clothes.

Just then, Emma sees Peg coming toward her. "I'm sorry Emma, the uniform is a deterrent and I must stay in uniform."

Emma couldn't believe her thoughts as she found herself thinking she would prefer to see Peg without any clothes on at all.

"Of course Peg, I'm so sorry, that was silly of me."

Peg didn't really call headquarters but she knew Emma would come to realize the necessity of being in uniform. And actually she heard people breathe a sigh of relief when they saw her stationed at the door. Most customers were aware that Emma's life has been threatened twice now and they wanted to continue coming into the store but were becoming concerned for their safety now, too. Many said they would continue to come to the store because they did fear someone did want to scare her out of business and they did not want to see that happen.

Chapter Thirty-Two

Bob contacts Alice and strongly suggests that she move more quickly because the deal needs to be made as soon as possible. The offer is high and the time is right and the corporation he is involved with wants the deal done now. And Bob stood to gain lots of money with the transaction.

"What do you suggest I do? She doesn't want to sell!" Alice was getting very tired of listening to his ranting.

"Well, I just thought you could talk to her and try to tell her that she stands to gain a lot if she sells. Just try to convince her to sell that property and then I'll sign the divorce papers.

"Oh that is just silly blackmail and I won't have any part of it," Alice turns her back to him to head out the door.

"I'm doing this for both of us!" he calls after her. "If you wouldn't have me setting the deal up you wouldn't even have had the chance to make three

times more than what the store is worth. You need
me!" decided Bob.

"With your help, I'll cut you in plus give you the
divorce you want," pleaded Bob, calling after Alice as
he watched her walk to her car and drive off.

Alice was through trying to reason with Bob. She
felt it was hopeless.

Chapter Thirty-Three

The bookstore sales are higher than they have ever been in the sales of books, drinks and food. It seems everyone wants to come in and listen to the ten minutes of fame open mic and also confirm that yes, there are reasons why a police guard should be stationed at the bookstore door. Emma spends long hours at the bookstore because she really didn't want to have to go home and face Alice.

Emma couldn't put her finger on it, but her trust in Alice was declining. It saddened her. She thought about seeing her attorney and having her will revised and leaving Alice some money but taking her out of the will that pertained to the bookstore. Emma thought that she would leave the bookstore to its true supporters: Tammy, Marie, Edie, Georgette and Frank, with the provision that they continue to run the bookstore as it is. But for some reason, call it a gut feeling, on her way to see her attorney she changed her mind.

Emma had just returned to the bookstore when she saw Peg at the door.

"Hey, how about some coffee?"

"I'm due to get off duty in about thirty minutes, how about something stronger at the bar across the street?" suggested Peg.

"Sounds good to me, I've had a trying day," revealed Emma.

Peg changed into street clothes. She takes Emma's hand and they find a small table in the back out of the traffic of customers and order two martinis from the waiter.

"I think this is just what the doctor ordered," said Emma taking a sip of her pomegranate martini.

"You're not on any medications are you?" asked Peg.

"No, probably should be; my head is full of suspicions and I lack trust," confessed Emma sadly. "This drink is the best medicine yet, and your company, of course."

"Suspicions? Sounds like a normal day for me in my line of work," Peg smiles as she takes Emma's hand. "Sorry honey, I don't mean to make your concerns small compared to mine." Emma smiles in return. Peg regrets her awkward attempt at comically breaking the ice.

"No," seriously, Emma, "I believe that that is totally applicable regarding the trauma, both physical and mental, that you have been going through lately. It's is totally understandable and I think it is amazing that you have endeared and can still run your business under these horrific conditions." Peg leans forward across the small table and touches Emma's cheek as she speaks.

"I think I need some advice," confesses Emma.

"Well, I am here for you, you know that," offers Peg.

"It's about Alice, either it is my imagination, or I feel her slipping away. I feel her mind is somewhere else lately," says Emma. "Oh, I know she has been busy with new clients and all, but there is just something that doesn't seem quite right."

"Like what?" searches Peg.

"She works late, every evening. I'm sure I am not contributing any to the situation either; but oh I just don't know. Something is really off. I'm sure she is affected also by all that has been going on."

"You are under stress and its true people do change. Just know that I am here for you and you can talk to me anytime about her or anything else. You know I care for you," Peg offers.

In her heart, Peg wouldn't mind Alice to be out of the picture. She realizes her assumptions are bias and of course she wants to find blame in Alice, so Alice does go away. She is being selfish and she knows it. Peg only knows that she is far too attracted to this woman sitting across from her to let go and not keep trying to win her love. With doubt she wonders what could this most attractive woman ever see in me, a rather short, slightly stocky, police officer. Her hair brilliantly white, her eyes dark and enduring that search my very soul, her skin olive and the perfect contrast to her hair. She's athletic, toned, and tall. How can I even go up against Alice who is in the same attractive league with Emma? Why am I even trying? Peg stops feeling bewildered, and gets back on track to listening to what Emma is saying that she needs from her now.

"I know the detectives are investigating further,

since the second incident," says Peg. "It's a wonder you manage at all."

"Well, I am frightened," admits Emma.

Emma and Peg are so busy talking that they do not notice the time is slipping away and it is now late into the evening.

"Oh, what time is it?" asks Emma. "I guess I should be getting home. I had a lovely time, promise we'll do it again soon."

"You know how I feel about you, Emma," confesses Peg as she holds Emma's hand. "I know you are going through a lot right now, just know that I am here for you and that I care deeply."

"Thanks, that means more to me than anything right now." Emma hugs Peg when they turn to leave the bar. "What's this?"

"Oh, I can wear my revolver off duty. We're allowed to do that."

Chapter Thirty-Four

It's late when Emma gets home. She sees the bedroom light on and that Alice is still awake, in bed reading and as Emma approaches she puts the book down.

"There you are, where have you been?" Alice wants to know.

"Oh, working late, guess the time got away from me." Emma found herself lying and was surprised at how easy it was to lie to Alice, someone she never thought of ever lying to. But lying came easy for some reason. She wasn't proud of this. Who was this Peg anyway, who suddenly popped into her life and seems to be pulling her and Alice further apart?

"That is unusual for you isn't it; and not to call? I feel that I haven't seen much of you lately, love," declares Alice. "Come here sit down and let me see how you are doing," Emma walks over to the bed.

"I was thinking the same thing. I thought you were trying to avoid me," says Emma.

"Well, I must confess, I haven't been home long, I've been busy, too."

Alice had worked into the evening with Bob mainly working on plans about the business. Bob felt that he was slowly winning Alice over to his side. He wanted to be friends with Alice. She didn't know it but his main goal was to try to get information from Alice about Emma's business. Personally to Bob, getting Alice back, was more of an important goal to him than even getting the bookstore property and was probably more of a reason that Charles could persuade Bob to work on Alice on getting information from Emma. All this was unbeknownst to Alice. She realized Bob was capable of some underhanded stuff but she never suspected any of this. She was just too naive and too trusting.

Emma feeling the relaxed arousal from the Martini slips in bed close to Alice.

"We should talk . . ." whispers Alice.

Alice's sweet smelling freshly showered hair moves Emma. She finds herself sliding even closer to her, leaning over her taking the book from her hands, reaches across her and putting the book on the night stand, in one smooth movement she takes that hand touches Alice's face, guiding her lips to hers. She pulls her close.

Alice returns Emma's kisses. Wrapped in each other's arms, they kiss, hands exploring, reaching tender sensitive breast that tingle and spark arousal. Silky nightclothes easily slide to the floor. Under the covers, hot with passion Emma kisses and touches smooth skin as fingers explore and Alice breathes hard in ecstasy. Alice moves down on Emma with sweet passion until she moans with delight. Sex was so overdue and so wonderful. Experiencing total bliss, each fully satisfied they lay in each other's arms in silence, in the dark, listening to each other breathe.

That night both women lie in bed pretending to be asleep. They both were feeling guilty, about not totaling trusting the other, but afraid to rock the boat at this point. Neither of them was sure of just how to approach the situation. Alice knew she was betraying Emma, yet for some reason Bob had this strong hold on her and she couldn't break free or confess to Emma the seriousness of Bob's scheming, or even grasp it the seriousness of it herself. She was in such denial. All she wanted was for him to sign the damn divorce papers and she'd be finally free of him.

Alice wanted Emma to still believe in her and to keep her trust. Alice didn't know if Bob had anything to do with Emma's accident and even if she thought he did, she couldn't prove it, but she expected as much, and was worried and becoming frightened.

****

The next day, Bob and Alice have a long conversation. Bob no longer wanted Alice to live with Emma. He doesn't like the idea of them sleeping together. He offered that maybe if she moved in with him, that he would then sign the divorce papers.

"You are sleeping with the enemy," professed Bob, "and I don't like it."

"Oh Bob, I am so tired of you and your excuses. The hell with the damn divorce papers; maybe if I'm a lucky woman I'll be a merry widow one day, the way your life is headed anything is possible," Alice retorted.

"Hey, are you threatening me?" Bob was getting angry.

Alice turned on her heel and was out of there. She had finally reached the tipping point.

"I'm through with this job, this silly job you offered me in return for your signature," Alice shouted. "I should have never agreed to this arrangement."

Chapter Thirty-Five

Marvin and Sam are on the case, checking out leads and trying to determine just who is behind all the attempts on Emma's life.

"Marvin, pull up over there and park," directs Sam.

"Why, what's up?"

"Let's get a smoothie!" suggests Sam.

"What?" asked Marvin who immediately begins to salivate at the thought of one of those wonderful delicious smoothies.

"I want to talk to Penny!" reveals Sam.

Marvin waited for a car to leave a parking place and parked the car down the street from the smoothie shop. They could see that the line of customers was out the door and lined up down the sidewalk along the building. It's so backed up that Marvin and Sam get dirty looks from those waiting as they try to squeeze their way through. They quickly give up the desire to use their official positions and resist the urge to pull out their badges, indicating official business, merely for the privilege of moving ahead of the line. They decide against it. Better not; they sheepishly take their place at the end of the line, all the while, avoiding angry eyes that said we don't care who you are, you have to wait in line just like everybody else!

"This is unreal!" whispers Marvin to Sam, their heads slightly bent down not looking around in fear of meeting the glaring eyes of those in line around them, ahead and behind them now. "Unbelievable, look at this line."

"What addictive substance is in those smoothies anyway, I mean I know they are good and all, but man, this women has a gold mine here." Detective Sam is sure something must not be on the up and up and mentally makes a note to have the ingredients checked out by a lab, being the suspicious detective that he is, never leaving a leaf unturned.

****

Suddenly there is an alert on their police radio that there has been a shooting nearby and Marvin and Sam should investigate. There a shooting victim, an attempted robber was killed, and an officer needs assistance.

"That's next door!" says Sam as a line of patrol cars zoomed by.

"That's next door!" echoes Marvin followed by an anxious sounding, "Come on let's get over there!"

"But our place in line . . ." trails Sam.

"Come on . . ." demands Marvin as he leads the way cutting in and out around people standing in line and moving up and around the long line past the entrance of the smoothie shop door and on ahead to see that the commotion is at the bookstore.

There were people everywhere, and the police quickly stretched a yellow crime scene tape to keep people back and protect the crime scene.

As Marvin and Sam fought to get through the crowd and went inside the sight that lay in front of them took them back.

Emma laid behind the counter on the floor, near her was the wounded shooter, white male, gun in hand, and lying in a pool of blood.

Emma had a bullet wound that apparently went through her shoulder and she was bleeding profusely and covered in blood. Peg, the officer who shot the attacker after the attacker shot Emma, was unhurt but shaken. Medics were on the scene hurriedly attending the injured and alerting the Trauma Center. Emma was barely conscious awaiting EMT transport and further examination at the Trauma Center. The shooter was unconscious and without identification.

Ambulance attendants had a difficult time getting the victims out past the news reporters who were interviewing the frantic regular customers of the bookstore, Edie, Georgette, Frank, and the others had witnessed the attack and shootings and each had different points of view and descriptions of what they thought they saw. It was obvious that police and reporters had their work cut out for them.

"We were all reading and having a bite to eat. Frank was setting up the mic for Open Mic time in the corner over there. Then we heard a scream and then gun fire," reported a very frightened and upset Edie. "Lord god what is this world coming to? See I tell you people are becoming more crazy." Of course, Edie's nervousness sent her on a "I'm talking and I can't stop," soap box tyrant about the evils of the world that will come down to being the fault of the one percent wealthiest in the world, who don't care about future generations, who run both parties in Washington and are out to start wars and coup d'etat takeovers for their own greedy profits and plans of global tyrannies.

"That woman, she's standing at the mic, yakking and she won't stop! She's like a motor that won't quit and she won't shut up even to come up for air!" exclaims Sam. "Like, this place is a zoo!" And no wonder with all the horrific commotion going on with another attempt on poor Emma's life.

Marvin looked about the exposed brick, big windows, and wide planked hardwood floor in the room. The room decorated with various floor plants that Marie and Tammy are dedicated in making sure they are well tended. In the corner off from the coffee bar and dining tables was a small platform with standing mic for Open Mic time. There stands Edie, arms wailing, preaching of the injustices of the world. They just let her rant and rave, the mic wasn't that loud and she wasn't hurting anyone, so why interrupt, let her go on with it, if it makes her feel better. There were rows of shelving and tables staked full of books between that area and the check-out registers near the door. So Sam wondered how the witnesses were getting a clear view of what had happened.

"So," imagines Sam aloud to himself. "He came in

the front door, picked up a book, walked over to the cash registers where Emma was working, then pulled out his gun."

Marvin joins in and continues the same thought pattern. "A customer saw the gun and screamed, alerting Emma and Peg," envisioned Marvin as he went on. "There was no ID on the unconscious man."

"We are awaiting word from the Trauma Center as to conditions and prognosis of the shooting victims."

"This is so tragic! Everything was so peaceful before Emma hooked up with that Alice woman," Marie told Marvin.

"What? Why blame Alice? By the way," wondered Marvin, "where is Alice?"

"Someone go find Alice . . ." demanded Marvin.

"Now Marie, Tammy tells me that you have always had a bad feeling about Alice, can you tell me just what do you mean by that?" inquires Marvin, searching for some sort of reasoning behind all of this chaos as of late.

"Well, Detective, Tammy may think that I'm a little of a wacko. But my gut tells me that Alice is up to no good and has been all along since she crept her way back into Emma's life. I don't think that it was any accident that Alice happened to rent an office near Emma and this bookstore. I think Alice is conniving and up to something, up to no good!"

"Can you give me more specifics?" pleaded Marvin, because so far, going on a "gut feeling" just isn't going to cut it in an arrest or stand up in a court of law.

"Well, I've seen those two together!" whispers Marie, hinting that she knows something but doesn't really want to let go of it, just yet.

"Who two?" asked Marvin.

"Why Alice and that 'man'!"

"Alice and what man? Tell me more," begs Marvin. This is like pulling teeth he thinks: just spit it out lady he wants to really yell but knows he has to "play the game" with this one.

"Can you tell me the name of the man?" asks Marvin whose face is turning red with frustration at this point.

"I believe, uh, his name is," says Marie, slowing as Marvin finds himself leaning ever more closer into Marie waiting on every breath to bring up some information. "Bob," she finally hissed, like hot steam from a leaky radiator.

"Bob, you say?" asked Marvin. "Was that him lying on the floor earlier?"

"Hmm, I thought that fellow looked familiar," Marie admitted. "Oh my!" She breathed suddenly feeling lightheaded as the events of the day catch up with her.

"Well," Marvin pleads thinking this is a losing battle and that this woman is wasting his time. "Can you tell me more?" he asked as he was reaching for a chair.

"Here sit down." He ordered as he takes her by the elbow and guides her over to the chair.

"Well, you know that very well could be the man I have seen Alice with from time to time. I have seen them together as I walked to work in the morning. I pass by her office to get to work. I can see in because the lights are on and it's still a little dark outside. For partners I thought they were rather chummy at times.

You know sitting rather close. Chummy partners I guess."

Marie is beginning to feel a little better as she sits down and retrieves a bottle of water from Tammy who has been watching from behind the food counter.

This information gets the wheels of thoughts and possibilities going on and turning in Marvin's head. It's hard to think however, because that woman, Edie, is still at it at the mic and no one has the heart or nerve to distract her and stop her, they merely turn the volume way down. She doesn't even notice. In her own way, endless chatter is her own neurotic way to release stress.

Chapter Thirty-Six

So most days, Edie continues chattering on and some people listen for a while then move on, some stand in a daze of disbelief or in amazement at agreement and belief.

"We are in a time of change people, let's face it. I believe as a society we have almost returned to the early industrial age of new productions and of greed. The greed is the same only in a larger scale where the one percent wealthiest own forty percent of all the wealth and that in itself is so powerful because they can control Washington. Both parties in Washington can, and I believe, are bought by them. The richest want to end the unions because they believe that the American people really do not want a union leader telling them how to vote. It's funny how they twist words and put edges on their meanings to suit their own goals and agenda.

They, both parties, have us fighting amongst ourselves to keep us distracted. The media, owned by the very few rich, puts out there what they want us to hear. We hear about all our potential enemies, leaders of other countries who do not treat their people right who have arms, as if we do not do the same. We all know that wars are started over the gaining of resources and making big profits for a handful of already very rich and powerful people. Personally, I don't care how people make their billions; however, I do care when their methods and ways are harmful to innocent people. Perhaps eventually we'll see a Global West and East division of leadership. Two leaders controlling the world, then what? I predict this by 2025 that is, if the world doesn't end before then. And I predict and rather hope that, if we do not have an to-end-all event, that we are somehow guided spiritually and lifted to a higher thinking, a higher consciousness where we all can communicate unilaterally in thought, share as a whole, as a group, our concerns for saving this great planet. It's catastrophic that the one percent seems to think the world was created solely for their own for-profit use. Ravishing the world's resources to use as they see fit for their own selfish monetary gain. And after they used it all up, then what? What if you ruled a planet you could no longer live on?"

She was not finished yet and so Edie continues. "Personally, I for one, believe it is the one percent who pooled their money and built a space craft in secret to transport themselves to a space station, I would guess near their home planet, Mars, home of the greedy, selfish, for-profit for themselves, few who rule and manipulate policy and the markets," Edie rants.

She is still not finished and continues, "The head federal bank is not a government owned bank but a bank that is owned by some of the biggest bankers and investors." To my knowledge this is what I believe..."

Edie goes on, "To my knowledge, the head federal bank holds the right to set interest rates and print money whenever they see fit. It sounds like it to me. Another thing that concerns me is the for-profit education and medical establishment that we live in. In Europe, yes, the taxpayers pay lots of taxes and we do too. Yes, those countries are in financial dire straits, but not any worse than we are. Are they in hock to China, too? Many people, comedians joke that we need to learn Mandarin. So amazing to me and I wonder if that one percent wonders how we are seeing things out here, in the real world."

And Edie still goes on, "There are collective agreements on what is happening. See, we're perhaps rising to a higher consciousness already. And then again one may think that, anyone would have to tune out and ignore the obvious if they do not see what is going on. Countries in Europe have near free education and practically free health care. Personally, and I can only speak personally, but for-profit health care sounds a little scary to me. The very sound of that scares me. That means to me that "they," the big shots, would not make any money, or certainly not billions over billions like they do now, if we are all healthy. We see commercial after commercial during prime time and really, all the time, throughout the day, pushing new diseases and their pills, to control that disease . . . never to heal. Oh yes, diet and exercise is key. Diet. Dieting is very interesting to me. Have you ever taken a road trip and all along that road trip is nothing to eat but junk food. Right? And the meat is raised — corn fed, not grass fed, in over-crowded, knee deep in waste feed lots. Yes, I've watched the DVD's we have here in the store on the subject. Did you know that cattle cannot digest corn and that it turns toxic in their gut? That I believe causes them to come down with e-coli. So cattle get lots the hormones too fatten fast and lots antibacterial shots to keep them alive, otherwise they would die before they are heavy enough to butcher. If they didn't kill them they would die anyway. So, it's a race to fatten them before they die. Can't blame them! After all, money is the root of all-evil isn't it? Amen to that!"

"They say our economy would come to a halt without oil. They say the end of the world could be caused by a sun flare knocking out the electricity on Earth in certain parts and it could be months before it is restored. Gas pumps will not be working without electricity; no nothing will be working. Okay, okay I know that I am blabbering, but this reminds me of Nikola Tesla, a scientist in the late 1800's, who got laughed out of town by the rich big shots who I believed own copper mines and wanted to run electricity current down copper wires into businesses and home where they could charge for electricity and make tons of money. Tesla got ridiculed and laughed out of town, because Tesla went against the grain and said that he could provide free electricity for everyone. Static electricity is everywhere. Isn't it amazing how a compass works with the magnetic pull of the North and South Poles? Obviously, Tesla had to be a big enough threat to the big shots, that they ridiculed him and laughed him out of town. We could all be driving electric cars. Which leads me, too. Did you know that cars in 1950—something could run 100 mpg with carburetor changed over that costs about fifty cents to alter? Yeah, some young no-body guy figured that one out and the big shot car manufactures bought the patent, calling him a genius and wished they have a guy like him on their team. The guy was told not to tell any more people about the patent or how to soup up their cars . . . well he did. Not long after, oddly coincidental, he had a fatal accident somewhere out in the desert. I saw it all on a DVD and by the way, you can buy that DVD here in the bookstore." Edie appears to be talking and cannot stop this morning... she continues on.

"Come on, you can't tell me that we can send rockets to space and not build a damn decent long life battery for an electric car. Did you know that light bulbs used to last a lot longer? There is no profit in that. I think folks found a light bulb burning way up high in an old barn. No one could reach it. It was still burning after about a hundred years. It was dim of course, but the filament never burned through. They don't make them like that anymore. And any of the swirling lights they make "green" are expensive, and very dim. Frankly I don't like them. As much as I read, honey, I need a decent light. So, I stay with the old style. Well, I have to! Another thing, remember how washers, dryers and refrigerators never wore out . . . not true anymore. Now you have to get the extended warranty, because you are going to need it. You think with millions of millions of more consumers these days, it would still pay to build quality products. Damn greed! Where's the integrity?"

"Another thing, I think and will probably hear a lot of flap about is that there is no profit in cures for illnesses; some of which are created in our minds by brainwashing television commercials followed immediately by a lawyer telling you that if you took a certain product and got diabetes or leukemia from it, then sue. Think about it!" This brought moans and boos from the small crowd having coffee and listening to her rant, which encourages Edie so she goes on. "It's like the big shots secret coups overthrowing governments and starting war for profits for a few." Edie only stopped preaching then, because she has something in her throat and starts coughing so Frank takes over.

"Well frankly," Frank says as he trades places at the mic with Edie, "I think it's all so messed up now with the government and the economy, and it can never be straightened out. That is probably why the elitist are ready to bail on us, build their space crafts and head up to their space station, I suspect is near Mars. Yes, they should go back where they belong—to Mars. I believe that mile wide spacecraft that folks are seeing over the southwest is a product of the rich elitist, and not an alien spacecraft. Come on, it's common sense, you can only buy so many jets, boats, houses, so why not pool billions together and build a spacecraft? And who knows with all the billions of dollars that the rich have, there could be more than one of those spacecrafts flying around in the southwest and other locations that people say they are seeing." Frank continues even after he sees that the crowd appears doubtful.

"Oh come on! We are talking egotistical men here who created god and the Bible to fit their own needs. There is a documentary about what I am saying. The store carries the DVD. Come on, a real god, would truly create all human being equally, don't you think? There would be no segregation, the racism, and the misogynism. I believe that the group of super-secret powerful people are a takeoff of the Roman Empire, creating god in their own image and likeness in order to control the masses."

Frank thinks of more to rant about, "And big chemical corporations want to spread their patented genetically altered with herbicides and insecticides seeds globally. I read that many countries are holding out, refusing to buy them but not for much longer, I'm sure. These companies are stationed all over the world. I once read in a book where, and I paraphrase, my intake and interpretation, of course, is that the president was overruled by big chemical corporations when he said Iran and other Middle Eastern countries we occupy did not have to buy these seeds. Big chemical thumped him and say that they are selling them and that these countries are buying them. Some countries still refuse. Like I said, I don't care what big rich corporations do globally as long as it is for the welfare of the people. Like that will ever happen. Men in powerful places need to get a conscious and work to benefit the people, for the good of all mankind and the planet. Where are the ethics? It's all about greed, it seems, these days! Don't officials and wealthy people have ethics to uphold? Whatever happened to trustworthiness, honor and integrity? Might as well toss those words right out of the dictionary. Yes, ethics, over taken by greed, and bought and sold to the higher corporate bidder, I'm guessing," says Frank.

Frank wraps up his ten minutes at the mic with,

"Well, that's how I see it and there are many books out there, I mean in the store here, that say the same thing. What goes on is for the big fat profits of a hand full of corporations that control our total food and water and drug supplies. Why are cancer treatment centers so crowded? One in four they say? Isn't that an epidemic? Why is it that they call surviving cancer for five years clean, then you survived, why five years? So, statically they can say they are curing cancer? Then they throw that statistic and record of that patient out; you know, juggle the records. They know it's probably going to return? You blast disease away with chemicals or radiation. What, kill that spot? Hello! The body contracts disease because it is not nourished well enough. Our foods are no longer nutritional; I don't think they are, anyway. I think that the human body needs sunshine and natural nutrition, like the happy cattle grazing on the green, rich grass, organic grass, from organic natural seeds, not mad scientist evil seeds, to grow and be happy and turn into non-nutritional meat. They also feed chemically blasted corn to farmed fish; we all know fish thrive better on algae, once again natural greens. If we had decent food, healthy foods we would all be healthy, the immune system would be healthy and fight off radical cells that might pop up, or not pop up at all. Then they tell us we all have cancer in us. Brainwashing us with commercials. The power of suggestion and self-fulfilled prophecy." Frank takes a breath and a drink of water and see that no one else wants to come up to the mic to speak about something, so he rants on.

"What we have here," continues Frank, "is a sad situation. The president in 1976 declared war on cancer.

People, whenever they say something like that, they are most likely setting you up for the very opposite scenario. And you can bet another money making scenario that benefits them, the rich elitist."

"I have seen extreme treatment as the patient goes through hell and in the end they lose the battle anyway. Not to compare life verses money spent. That's the unthinkable. The trick here is, they preach god, the Bible, they tell us we are sinners, needing god, so we obey and behave. But the whole time we are being conditioned not to suspect that human beings making big profits would keep people hanging on until their every last dime is spent. And in the end losing the battle anyway. We think everyone is as morally holy as each of us are. Even the innocent working in the fields is handed down demands: push this pill, push that pill, get kids on pills and start them out at a very young age and condition them that being sick some way or another and on medication is the natural course of life. And it's all for greedy profits?" Frank was really raging war now!

Still Frank continues on he can't do anything about his son's kidney, and it seems getting up and blasting the industry helps. He goes on, "On that one I know you all will come up here and haul me away from this mic. What causes cancer? Crap for meat, crap disposed of in the water supplies. Don't know what to do with the extract from manufacturing aluminum, hell, dump it in the drinking water, and call it fluoride and say that it prevents cavities. So I've heard, can't prove it, but that is what I've heard. They, the big shots, don't care about us, they only care about lining the top executives pockets. Anymore, with all the greed, the heads of corporations make over four-hundred times more than their employees and it seems they still want more."

Frank is getting hoarse now, but continues with his rant. "I know, it's scary out there, the atrocities that mankind performs on each other. It's scary! To think dropping bombs on innocent people is okay? For what purpose I ask? Is it to conquer, and to knock out the competition; to teach somebody a lesson, and to show your might and dominance? It sounds childish to me. Seriously, sometimes I think that I have landed on the wrong planet. Men espoused religion, oh, I don't care what sect, but men are better than women, badger women, torture them, hold them down; they do this to other men too. Why? What ugliness lies within the soul of such evil acts? I suspect it's what happened to the planet, Mars. Mars once had life on it. I suspect a testosterone charged society of evil spirits ravished that planet. The forces of good and evil! It's certainly not balanced. There is only a handful of evil . . . those who do harm to others in the sense of greed and power and super profits. For what, I ask you? You can't take it with you. If evil would suddenly be turned into love, how wonderful would that be?" And with that, Frank wipes his eyes and returns to his favorite big comfy chair. But not before getting back up to the mic and thanking Emma, "May the healing spirits be with her so she recovers quickly."

At this point, Georgette, introduced her friend Rosy a first timer. Rosy seems a little nervous to be at the mic but speaks her mind clearly, "The indigenous peoples of this Earth, all around this Earth had the right spirit;

they were connected to the star people; they worshiped Mother Earth, Mother Nature and lived off the land and replenished and nourish the land and each other. There was peace. We ravish the Earth and do not put back. The rich only take for themselves, only for their greedy selves. There must be a profit in it. I think that there is something terribly wrong with that! Scientist like to make out that they are god like in trying to figure out the planets, the universe, the galaxies; they have no idea what is out there, because they are too egotistical to see the love connection; that we are all connected and that the world could be the "perfect" place if only greed were not a factor." Rosy confidence increases as more people sit down to listen and so she continues.

"Why is there greed? Why are we so weak in self-esteem that we have to punch out the other guy in the face, and stomp on our mothers to get the brass ring? It's sick. And people this is what happened here today, this shooting, this attack, is only a microcosm of the macrocosm that goes on throughout the patriarchal world and it's all over. This sick anger and greed is everywhere! We are destroying each other and the Earth over evil greed . . . and now okay, okay, I see the store is closing. Thanks for listening. Guess I got a little carried away." And Rosy steps aside as Georgette gets back on the platform to speak.

"I just want to thank everyone again for this open mic platform. It helped so immensely today after what has taken place in the store. We are all traumatized at the shooting. This is our way of distressing this horrific event. I am sure that I speak for everyone when I say that our thoughts and prayers are with Emma. She has been going through some terrible experiences recently. A true mystery! We feel helpless but not hopeless and know that she will be fine as we turn our thoughts and our positive energies her way. Thank you." And with that Georgette steps down.

Throughout the day, Tammy and Marie had kept them posted on Emma's improving condition. They are still in shock.

Edie preaches as she looks around the darkened room, past the floor lights of the platform that she stands on and sees that there is no one there to listen except the cleaning crew . . . one or two applaud as Edie steps down and heads towards the doors and off into the night heading home with her arms full of books to read late into the night to come back again if not tomorrow, the next day, but probably tomorrow, to regurgitate what she has read, again to another silent, non-listening crowd.

Chapter Thirty-Seven

Havoc was occurring in the Trauma Center ever since the shooting victims were brought in.

A nurse, who knows Emma and Alice, called Alice who had just arrived and was speaking with the nurse. A police officer who identified the shooter through bar codes on a key chain gym membership card, called Alice because the shooter had Alice's name and cell phone number as a contact in case of emergency.

Alice had the look of shock on her face and was running back and forth, taking the elevator between floors checking on the shooter and then the victim, puzzling police, patients and hospital staff. While heading to the elevator, moving most uncomfortably between patients as detectives Marvin and Sam approached her.

"Mrs. Johnson?" asked Marvin. "You are Mrs. Bob Johnson ,are you not?"

"Yes, I am," Alice admitted looking shaken and confused.

"And you are the romantic and business partner of Emma Kingston?" Marvin pressed on.

"Yes I am!" Alice admitted obviously very shaken.

"Just what is going on here?" asked Sam.

"I don't know." And Alice began to cry. Sam hands her a handkerchief. He can't help but feel a little sorry for her.

It appeared to be a jealous husband shooting. Upon further questioning, Alice reveals that Alice and Bob were not divorced because he would not sign the divorce papers unless she would get Emma to sell her bookstore property. Alice said she had told Bob forget it then I'll stay married. She knew Emma would never sell the bookstore.

****

Alice, is distraught, and torn apart by feelings of guilt. Now she is left with nothing. How did this all begin. Her thoughts are rambling and driving her crazy. She always tried to be a good person, a good Catholic raised girl. She always did what she was told and tried to please everyone else. Her mother was cold her father was distant; she grew up on a little farm with an older abusive brother. The boys in the neighborhood were just mean and chased and punched her. Boys got away with everything. Boys were always right. Boys will be boys was the excuse her mother gave. She grew to hate boys and the special treatment and advantages they got.

No wonder, she thought, she had crushes and special feelings for other girls. Alice just couldn't see how girls were boy crazy and chased after them. Why? They were mean and dominant. Society called it being a gentleman, but Alice saw it has being controlling and domineering. Alice's cold and non-emotional mother was no help. When Alice was a toddler at her mother's knee reaching up to her, wanting to be picked her up and held, her mother pushed her away saying, "You're too big to hold." Little Alice was devastated and heartbroken; her father, just as cold, had only laughed at the sight of her mother's coldness. Alice was actually afraid of him.

Alice's life was spent trying to please her mother; she hoped in turn her mother would love her. There is no such thing as love her dad would say. And when she asked her mother why they got married, she angrily responded as it was after one of her parents' many arguments, "Because we were in love." Her dad only snarled and said "love" in a discouraging way as if love were a sickness, a weakness, something to be ashamed about.

In Alice's world, men were cold and men were cruel and abusive. She learned at a very young age that life was going to be a long hard road. She knew she never wanted to get married, she knew that at a very young age. She told her mother one day when she was about twelve that she was never going to get married. "Well, you're supposed to!" her mother angrily shot back.

And it was just the way her mother said and many times you have to do what was expected of you and not particularly what you may have chosen to do for yourself.

Alice remembered another time when she was

very young, about four or five, asking her emotionally detached mom who seemed so distant and her life such a drudgery, "Why did you have kids?" She wanted to hear her mother say, because we love children and we couldn't wait to have you. But that wasn't her mother's answer, "Well, we wanted a boy first to help dad in the fields with the farm work and then we wanted a girl to help me with the work in the house." Alice was heartbroken.

This is what Alice remembers of her childhood. She also remembered her dad putting his hand on her bare knee on the way to school one day as she sat next to him, while he drove her to school. She didn't remember anything else after that only that it felt wrong. From the time she was a baby he never held her like she seen other daddies do their kids.

Looking back, unlike today, there were no social services back then for kids, certainly not in small towns. It seemed that men set themselves up in powerful positions, and taught people to respect and honor authority, and then took advantage of those powerful positions. As soon as Alice was old enough she was on her own. She wanted to get a job and be financially independent and work her way through college. It took a while to get through college but timing is everything and it's where she met Emma, through Bob, on a double date.

Bob told Alice marrying him would be the best thing for her and the way Emma, acted when she was around, just wasn't right. "What will people think?" he asked. Just like her mother always asked, "What will people think?" To Alice's mother, it was very important what other people thought. Appearances were everything. Apparently, however, Alice's thoughts and needs were unimportant. Anyway, that was how Alice interpreted it; other people were always more important and always knew better. And, then of course, women were considered to be secondary citizens and socialized and conditioned to love, honor and obey their men, something that never sat well with Alice.

Alice's heart was broken when she as a small girl and she realized she had no escape from the so-called norms of society. Depressed over the thought of such a patriarchal, authoritarian future she knew back then as a kid that she was never going to be able to live life as she dreamed of living it. She knew too that she was destined to be under some man's thumb, that's just the way it was.

But, Alice loved women, especially kind, warm-hearted women. Any woman who was kind to her, she loved. She became even more shy and it made her want to cry. She was starved for affection.

****

Emma was sweet and kind, and Alice was blown away the moment she met her. But the ideas of guilt and shame Bob threw in her face brought up all those old strict teachings of her childhood. So Alice went along with his plan half-heartedly. "Because you're supposed to" tapes played in her head. Alice was confused. It's hard to know how to receive and give love when you never experienced love the way other people experience love. The pains of childhood can last a lifetime.

Alice felt that she set Emma up for her attack and for that she was truly sorry, and felt that she did not deserve her love or understanding. She was afraid, but felt that whatever consequences would come from her actions, she deserved.

Chapter Thirty-Eight

Alice heard Peg in the hospital room speaking to Emma, handing her a sip of water while she holds the glass and straw for her.

"Peg, to the rescue," whispers Emma. "I love you for it."

"I thought you loved me my blue eyes," smiles Peg.

"Those, too." Emma smiled back and Peg leaned over and kissed her forehead.

"Well here I am again, when is this fiasco ever going to end?"

Alice slipped away, as an officer came on duty to guard Emma's room.

"Has Alice been here?" Emma asked Peg.

"I think she was here earlier when you were unconscious."

"Emma, there is something I need to tell you. And I hate to be the one, but you should know."

"Know what?" asked Emma, sounding tired and hesitant.

Peg figured she just as well come right out with it. She took a deep breath...

"The man who shot you is Alice's husband!"

"Husband? You mean Bob?" Emma rubs her forehead that is beginning to ache.

"They are not divorced," Peg tells her.

"Oh, I know that. Alice has told me that Bob won't sign the divorce papers," acknowledged Emma and then adds, "oh, no wonder Alice is not here." Emma's heart sinks. Emma remembered Alice telling her that Bob wouldn't sign the divorce papers.

"Why did he shoot me then—jealousy?" asked Emma trying to make sense of it all as she looks into Peg's eyes.

****

It's been a very difficult time for Emma, all the attempts on her life and not knowing what for or for certain that each attempt was meant for her alone. And learning that people she thought she could trust are not to be trusted. Did Bob try to kill her out of jealousy or was there more to this.

Chapter Thirty-Nine

"Damn, does this women have nine lives?" curses Bob as he hears the cop at his hospital room door and the nurse talk about the victim being alive and doing well. "Damn!"

The plan was to run into the store, pretend to hold up the store and make sure Emma was killed in the process. Bob was losing patience; the hit man could not get rid of her so he had to try to do the deed himself. Damn! He wanted that bookstore location, there were rumors that in a few years a giant hotel and shopping conglomerate were planning to buy out that area and develop there. Also, he not only wanted that bookstore location, he needed it, and his life depended on it. Bob was in hock up to his eyeballs to loan sharks that were threatening his life. He needed collateral and bargaining power.

Emma's parents were rich, sitting on a gold mine location, and that big chain company offered her parents millions if they would sell out. They wouldn't, so Bob arranged their airplane crash. Bob knew that Alice was in love with Emma, so he played it up. He moved his office near the bookstore in hopes that Alice and Emma would get together again. His plan worked. But Alice was supposed to be in the store, too. He could have gotten both of them at one time, which would have been less suspicious. That is what the hit man was supposed to do, but he kept screwing up.

It had been obvious that Bob was going to have to take care of business himself, so he had tried. Alice was in Emma's will. Since Emma had no relatives, with both of them out of the way at one time, he would inherit what Alice would have gotten from Emma. If only it would have happened as planned. He cursed to himself and had to figure out his next move.

Chapter Forty

Alice realized Bob was using her when she realized she was supposed to be in the store with Emma. "He set me up, that son-of-a-bitch!" Alice at the last minute had remembered a dental appointment so was not there. Otherwise she would have been shot, too.

Alice was afraid to face Emma. She knew her hesitation to do so spoke volumes, she was afraid and now realizing the truth made it all the more difficult. Alice saw Peg leaving Emma's hospital room as she rounded the corner of the hall.

As she approached the room, she noticed the officer at Emma's door had stepped away to speak on his cell phone. She slipped into the room as his back was turned. Not quite knowing where she would fit into all of this, she was worried, *Will the police tie her in with her husband?*

"Alice," Emma said in total surprise not knowing what to think, not even knowing anymore how to feel. Her heart jumped when she saw Alice but she wasn't quite sure what her response to her presence should be since Alice's husband just tried to kill her.

"Emma, are you okay?" Alice moved close to the bed and saw the bandages. "Oh my god what...?" She was speechless.

Emma just wanted to cry. She was confused and didn't know if she could trust Alice's judgment anymore. She loved Alice but Alice's actions and her own feelings were confusing her.

"I had no idea . . ." Alice sat down next to the bed and buried her face in her hands and cried. "I'm so sorry." She repeated over and over again. "I'm so sorry." She wanted to come close to Emma and hold her, but she was afraid to. She blamed herself for Bob's attack on Emma.

"Were you two seeing each other?" Emma asked Alice.

"It's true, as we worked more and more together he wanted to keep the marriage intact and wouldn't give me a divorce," cried Alice.

"So you were sleeping with him?" asked Emma. "Is that what set him off to come after me?" Emma demanded to know.

"I was supposed to be working in the store this morning, too, remember?" urged Alice.

It was true, since Alice's consulting business was slow in building she was working a couple a days a week helping Emma out in the store.

"So, you think he was deranged and wanted to get both of us. Maybe so, but you set him off, sleeping with him! And that's why he wouldn't sign the divorce papers?" demanded Emma.

Emma's shoulder was aching, and her head was hurting from trying to make sense out of just what has been going on in the past few weeks. Why would Alice's husband come after her and not Alice, if he were so jealous of Alice living with her? She was confused. The detectives were suggesting that Charles, Bob and Alice were working together to get the property because they stood to make millions in a real estate deal. Finally, Emma just had to close her eyes and remove herself from it all and Alice silently left the room still crying.

Chapter Forty-One

Being inseparable, Marie and Tammy were working the cash register together. Several of the regulars joked that they were conjoined twins because where one was, the other was. Their hair was styled the same, and they dressed alike. They said they just both happened to have the same taste. "It happens a lot in lesbian couples!" they would say.

Marie and Tammy, saw just about everything through the same set of eyes, and most of the time they spoke sweetly to each other but this morning could be heard bickering, by Edie and Frank as they sat at a nearby table in the snack area.

"I told you I didn't trust Alice! She's no better than that jerk of a husband, Charles, that Emma had! When he was working here, he was cooking the books," said Tammy. "It's a wonder we weren't all killed by that nut head!" Tammy went on.

In between working the cash register, waiting on

customers and serving up coffee, Marie and Tammy really didn't have a lot of time to talk and figure all this mess out, for business had doubled in the last day or so since the gunman came into the store. You'd think the opposite would be true that people would be afraid to hang around knowing that now gun shooters hung around the place. But no matter how infamous the bookstore might have become, it seems that there were more reporters and cameramen interviewing customers every day, which drew people in at the chance of being in the newspaper or on television. The bookstore was becoming as busy as the smoothie shop next door. People would come and visit both places; it was the most popular tourist attraction in the area.

Marie and Tammy weren't dummies and saw the opportunity early on to add more outside tables with umbrellas, as did the smoothie shop. Business was booming in the neighborhood. Marie and Tammy hired extra help for the second time in the last six months.

"You know, maybe Alice is a good thing after all," realized Tammy.

"Yeah, it might be better for us if we went a little easier on Alice. Yes, I agree that she is naive and gullible, however, Emma likes her." With some reservation Marie hesitantly agreed.

Right after Emma's parents died and before Alice came back into Emma's life, Emma had put Marie and Tammy into her Revocable Trust as beneficiary in case something would happen to her.

Alice had always had a place in Emma's heart; but, at the time of her parents' death Alice was not in

Emma's life, and not in her will much at all, just a few of Emma's assets would go to Alice. The majority of the business would go to Marie and Tammy.

After Emma's parents died in the plane crash, Emma became suspicious of Charles business tactics and divorced Charles. So he was cut out of all her business matters. But, he continued to drag her into court in an effort to get half of everything, which would mean, selling the business. So, at that time, Emma moved more of the business matters in her will to Marie and Tammy.

Through the years Alice and Emma drifted apart, then Emma divorced Charles and Alice separated from Bob. But Bob and Charles had always remained friends, and business associates. Both men realized from early on that Emma's parents' bookstore business was prime real estate. What the men knew, and Emma did not know, was that the property was worth much more than what Emma thought it was worth. To Emma, the bookstore had sentimental value; and she wanted to hang on to it; she didn't really care about the money. But to Charles and Bob, who were greedy, and saw the monetary value, the property was worth killing someone over. After all, accidents do happen.

Chapter Forty-Two

"So the worm has turned! Marie and Tammy know they are in the will, and know that Alice is out of the will. Could Marie and Tammy be letting Alice and Bob do their dirty work for them?" Marvin wonders aloud.

"Oh come on, I've had enough of this, now we are dragging them into the mess of suspects?" argued Sam.

"Well, think about it, they have nothing to do but just let the whole damn thing play out!" suggested Marvin then added, as it suddenly occurred to him. "Maybe Charles is in cahoots with Marie and Tammy? Let's find out more about how they got to know each other and how they had come to get their jobs in the bookstore," suggested Marvin.

"Jeez, I need a smoothie, can we get a smoothie first, at least!" whined Sam.

"Okay, let's get in the car and head on over there. I want to talk to Marie and Tammy, separately," demands Marvin eager to get to the bottom of all this.

It's a beautiful warm spring morning, the birds are chirping, the flowers in the store front boxes are blooming, the freshly trimmed grass smells divine as Marvin and Sam pull up in front of the smoothie shop, park the car and proceed to stand at the end of the long line that has already formed outside the shop door, along down the sidewalk.

"Think I'll get a banana strawberry smoothie this morning," says Sam practically salivating just thinking about it.

"Okay, I am going to reach out and try a different flavor this morning. Personally, I'll be glad when this case is over; I think I have gained ten pounds stopping by here all the time on the way to the bookstore," grinned Marvin while patting his protruding belly.

"Yeah, maybe you just dreamed up that excuse about questioning Marie and Tammy just so you could stop by the smoothie shop," smiled Sam.

"You never know. But let's think about it and follow the money. Who stands to gain the most? Certainly not Charles, he's not even in the will. What if Marie and Tammy cut him in just to do their dirty work for them?"

"Well, you certainly have a point there, and a valid motive," admits Sam. As he sticks the straw in his giant size, thirty-two ounce smoothie as Marvin looks on at Sam's expanding waistline, rolls his eyes, and smiles.

Sam sees Marvin's look and says, "Just thought we might not be back for a while, so I got the big one!"

They both had to laugh at that.

"A heart attack waiting to happen." As he turns and looks at Sam then turns back to the waitress at the counter and says. "Oh hell, give me the same size, too! The big one!"

And Marvin and Sam are off to a good start of their day. They drink half their smoothies strategizing how their interview with the two ladies should go.

"Remember, the day of the shooting how Marie was so upset and wasn't quite sure that was Bob lying on the floor and then decided that it was?" pointed out Marvin.

"Yeah, right away she pointed the finger at Bob, knowing that the accusation would include his wife, Alice, whom Tammy says she never had a good feeling about, remember?" added Sam.

Stuffed and deciding to finish the smoothies later, they were anxious to get into the bookstore to further question Marie and Tammy. As they entered they saw that both Marie and Tammy were busy stocking books on shelves, then Tammy headed to register to check out a customer.

"Good morning, Marie! Man, you ladies are working hard. Looks as if you could use more help around here these days."

"We sure could use more help, you got that right, detective. What can I do for you this morning?" asked Marie, reaching into a box and pulling out four books at a time in each hand.

"Well, Marie, we just have a few more questions to ask if you don't mind. We'll try to make it brief seeing how busy you are," stated Marvin.

"What is it that you need to know?" asked Marie as she stepped away then back to the big box of newly arrived books after stocking the shelves and sounding a little out of breath.

"Well, just some background information, like when you began working here and how did you come to know Tammy. Did she already work here? Did you both know each other before hand? Just things like that if you don't mind," asked Sam.

Marie went ahead and began answering his questions while she continued to unload boxes. "Well, I got the job here about eight or nine years ago, when I got laid off from my other job in a chain bookstore. Bookstore business is what I know, but I was tired of the big chain bureaucracy, so I thought I would check out an independent bookstore to try to get work.

Coincidentally, Tammy worked at the big chain store too and was laid off with me and so she applied here soon after I did. Emma hired us on the spot when we were in here one day when Emma, poor thing, was swamped with customers. She needed help after her parents were no longer here to help her run the store, and we both had experience, which came in mighty handy. I don't mind saying so myself," bragged Marie.

"So, that's very interesting. Well, you certainly seem like dedicated employees. I am very impressed from what I've seen of your work ethics." Sam was smoothing the way.

"Well, we aim to stay here as long time if at all possible, we like the family, fun atmosphere here, and Emma has always treated us well."

"Just have to ask another question, if you don't

mind," asked Sam. "And that is, is there any kind of partnership or ownership status between you, Tammy and Emma?"

"Well, after her parents died, her lawyers suggested someone be added to Emma's will, just for safe keeping, in case anything happened to Emma, and Marie and I were added. Just to keep things updated I guess." Marie was beginning to hesitate with her answers wondering where all these questions were headed.

"That would be a big leap for you two, wouldn't it, if something should happen to Emma, you two would have to take over the whole store. Since you're in the will and all."

"Well, I guess we could do that, we both have business degrees and bookstore background, although it would be tough. I guess we just never thought that anything would ever happen to Emma," claimed Marie.

Tammy returned from waiting on a customer and working the register to help Marie empty boxes of books and stack the shelves as Marvin and Sam continued to ask questions. At this point the detectives didn't know what to think. The two ladies certainly had a lot to gain being the sole inheritors. After a while, Sam and Marvin bid the ladies farewell and strolled out of the store. Once outside, Sam had a thought.

"You know the timing all seems to be coincidental, doesn't it, I mean, between the time Emma and Alice got together, and Emma's parents died, and Marie and Tammy got hired. Don't you think Marvin?" Not waiting for Marvin's reply Sam goes on, wrapped in his own thoughts.

"Interesting," admits Sam as they walk to their car.

"With Emma out of the way, there is no longer a sentimental reason to keep the bookstore . . . I think that is the most important issue. Emma had thoughts of turning it in to a co-op but lawyers advised her to do a Revocable Trust leaving the store to Marie and Tammy," acknowledged Marvin as he slid into the driver's seat.

"Let's head to the records department again and check out the name of the lawyer on that will and see if he is connected in any way with anyone else that is involved in all of this," suggested Marvin as he turns the key to start the car.

****

"Well, what did those two want again, Marie?" asked Tammy when she finally got a little break from going back again to the register and over to help Marie unpack yet another box of books.

"Oh, seems we are moving up on the lists of suspects," suggested Marie.

"Did they actually say that?" Tammy's eyes grew big as she cocked her head in disbelief.

"No, but they know, we know that they know, we are in the will!" says Marie. "And really if you think about it, Alice doesn't really know that she is out of the will, does she?" submits Marie as she bent over to slice open the top of a box of books with her box cutter.

Chapter Forty-Three

"What are you doing here?" demanded Bob from his hospital bed. "Dressed like an orderly, well aren't you clever, with an ID even. Where'd you get that anyway?" Bob asked calmly. But then he doesn't like the look in Charles' eyes and he begins to become alarmed and squirms around nervously on the bed.

"Well looks like you are recovering rather nicely," observes Charles smiling ever so slightly. "Maybe I should check your vitals while I'm here!" He devilishly grins and thinks to himself—*or adjust them, like cut them off.*

"Like I asked, what are you doing here? You'll blow our cover," demands Bob.

"I'll blow our cover, look who got himself shot and put in the hospital. Have they questioned you yet?" Charles wanted to know.

"Yeah, they have, they are treating it like a domestic issue of jealously and rage," declared Bob.

"Well, how convenient!" Charles snaps. "Guess

I can't kill you just yet. But you could die from complications of some sort, don't forget that."

"You ass! What about Emma, she's on the next floor, wouldn't it be more beneficial for you to get her out of the picture? After all she is the one who is keeping us from getting our hands on that property by refusing to sell," quipped Bob but sounding more like he was pleading as he squirmed as far as he could towards the edge of the bed away from Charles.

"That is why we have to be very careful of how we get rid of her, so we are not suspected," suggests Charles.

"Yeah, too bad you're going to be sitting in jail over an assault charge if you touch me!" Bob points out looking more nervous and wondering why he said that only to get Charles upset.

"Hey! You know I know good lawyers and judges, who love to be cut in on a good deals!" bragged Bob.

"So you do?" snapped Charles.

"Hell yeah! You don't think I would miss out on being part of a sweet deal like this do you, and even if I were in jail, I should get my share. Hey I can work from jail. No problem!" boasts Charles.

"Oh, I'll make sure you get your share," insisted Charles seething with silent rage. "I'll make sure you get your cut alright," Charles says as he suddenly jerks the pillow out from under Bob's head and forcefully pushes it down hard on Bob's face. Bob begins struggling to breathe, his arms flailing, legs kicking.

Bob's yells are nothing more than mumbles as his cries for help are muffled and go unheard, yet he continues to struggle under Charles' weight and strength. Bob struggles but is weakened by the bullet wound.

Charles is spent and can barely push down much longer. "Die damn you," Charles commands. "I'm wearing out here!" With one last hard push on the pillow, the deed is done.

"Jesus!" Finally Bob stopped struggling and became still and silent. "Finally! Jeez! I worked up a damn sweat!" crabbed Charles. And complained even more as he prepared to leave the room, "Got my scrubs all sweaty." Charles continues to complain under his breath as he quietly steps around the room preparing to leave, but not before sneaking a peek around the corner of the open door to see if the guard is still sitting outside the door.

The guard is sitting outside the door but hears nothing, nor notices that the beeping of the heart monitor screen has just come to stillness.

Charles quickly puts the pillow back under Bob's head again so it looks like he just innocently expired. Charles gets behind the cart he pushed into the room and pushes it out of the patients' room into the hall in front of the door, pushes it down the hall and leaves it sit, after he rounds the corner. He grabs the bag containing his clothes from underneath the cart. No one is even remotely suspicious. Coming in the middle of the afternoon was the perfect time to come visit a patient, as suggested by a friend who was an orderly. Charles had asked his friend when was the best time to visit a friend in the hospital that wasn't the busiest. He changed his clothes in a rest room stall and walked out into the hall to the elevators carrying the bag.

On his way out of Bob's hospital room, Charles very cleverly, he had to admit even to himself, decided to put a kink in Bob's oxygen hose by pitching it in one of the brackets of the stand, so it looked like a hospital error and a case of negligence. Which will most probably get covered up and Bob's death will be recorded as death due to complications of his injuries. Charles will no longer have to worry about Bob spilling his guts. Nor will he have to worry about giving Bob a part of the cut once the deal was complete.

Charles got in the elevator and out of it on the floor where Emma's hospital room was located; it pays to have a friend who owes you money who works in the hospital and who can check admissions in order to find which room a patient is staying in. It's just so much nicer than having to call the information desk. Charles has to smile, this was so easy and he was so damn smart he could barely stand himself.

Charles rounds the corner to head for the restroom to change back into the scrubs, when he sees several uniformed police officers standing near a room talking, but wait, it looks like they may be ready to disperse. Charles is getting a little nervous and would like to get the deed over with while he still has the nerve because this one is more personable. Charles is angry because he could not win the store through the divorce. Charles slips into the rest room to change.

Chapter Forty-Four

"See you guys later," Peg calls after the officers who were leaving.

"Thanks for taking over, Peg. Let us know when we can return the favor," says one of the officers as they head towards the elevator.

"And don't you look sexy in your uniform!" flirts Emma, as Peg bends down to kiss her sweetly on the lips.

"Woo, another kiss like that and I'll be healed!"

"Okay then, my love! Another kiss it is."

"Hmm, I like," smiles Emma. "You know I have never officially thanked you for standing guard in the store that day and for saving my life."

"Well, chances are, if I would have had been on duty and would have had on my uniform, he never would have stepped foot into the store to begin with, and none of this would have happened."

"Well, we'll never know that, besides he could have

come through the back entrance if he really wanted to," admits Emma.

"Nevertheless, it was the customers who saved you by screaming so loud, which got my attention and also threw his aim off. You can thank them. But if it makes you feel better I can think of lots of ways for you to thank me when you feel better and you get out of here," Peg smiles and flirts as she straightens Emma's pillow then looks around to see what else needs to be done to make her more comfortable.

"Oh, your water pitcher is empty," Peg notices. "I'll fill it for you."

"Out of the bathroom tap should be okay, I have plenty of ice left," said Emma as she lays her head back on the pillow and closes her eyes to rest them while Peg goes in the bathroom.

Peg turns around from the bed with pitcher in hand and heads into the bathroom. Just then Charles comes around the corner in the hall and doesn't see an officer at Emma's door. At first, he wonders if they had moved her or if she had been released from the hospital already. He was back in scrubs complete with ID and a stethoscope looped around his neck.

Charles peeks in the room and sees Emma. She is alone and just lying there apparently sleeping. He is eager to get it over with and so he goes in and being in a hurry and nervous, he clumsily bumps into the service tray next to her bed.

"Crap!" he mutters under his breath as he nervously catches himself and grabs the tray to keep it from rolling into something else and making even more of a racket.

Hearing the noise, Emma is startled awake and looks up in surprise and gasped aloud.

"What are you doing here?" she says in a low voice almost angrily. She continues, "Why are you dressed like that?" Her eyes growing wide as she begins to feel threatened by his odd and sudden appearance at the foot of her bed but moving up closer to her face.

"I'm tired of you asking questions!" he seethes through his teeth. Blood already on his hands after killing Bob, he is angry and in a wild state of mind, and wants to shut her up fast.

She's whining now just like Bob did. "I can't stand that whining." He rushes to her bed and yanks the pillow from behind her head before she even realized what was happening. He then forces it past her waving hands over her face and pushes her down back onto the bed, hard. Harder and harder he pushes his eyes glazed in an insane daze. Emma struggles, her arms waving and legs kicking she successfully knocks the bed cart with her foot and it goes flying against the medal standing lamp making a crashing sound. Emma hopes it's loud enough to get Peg's attention. It works! Upon hearing the crash, Peg comes flying out of the bathroom leaving the water picture behind in the sink.

Peg sees the man's back, his head is down, he is wearing scrubs but something is terribly wrong. She whips out her revolver from her side holster and moves around slightly where she can see that he is trying to smother Emma.

She yells, "Freeze!" It's like the attacker is in a mad trance! He pushes harder and harder. His face is red, his hair hanging in his face, wet with sweat. Emma's arms are beginning to relax. She stops struggling.

Peg circles around the bed to face the attacker. She is startled at the sight of the man and his unbelievable rage. Who is this man? She's never seen anything like this before. In an adrenaline rush, she fires her weapon hitting him dead in the chest. Peg doesn't know whether to scream or cry, her hands are shaking at the sight of the dying man. Charles has the look of shock and surprise in his eyes as he stares at Peg while he slumps, sinks to his knees, and slides down the side of the bed onto the floor. Dead.

Peg rushes to reach the bed to where she can get to Emma and remove the pillow from her face. She grabs it and slings it across the room. She's crying as hospital personnel upon hearing the shot come rushing in.

Emma begins choking and coughing, Peg had gotten to her just in time and tries to raise her head a bit so she can straighten out and get more air in her lungs. Slowing Emma gets her wind back and is able to breathe without choking and coughing.

"Hang in there," Peg whispers as she waits and watches as do the hospital workers joined now by police. And Emma begins to recover from yet another attack on her life. It's all like a bad nightmare; will it ever end?

"I don't know how much more of this shit I can take!" Emma finally blurts out in anger. "I've had enough! Jesus!"

"I know it's hard but try to calm down a bit, so you can breathe without hyperventilating," a doctor suggested.

The hallowed halls echoed the sound of the gunfire and soon the room fills with even more hospital staff and police officers coming from all directions. Charles is pronounced dead at the scene.

Peg gives a full report while Emma is given a mild sedative and oxygen to help her breathe. The doctors tell Peg that Emma is going to be all right. Well physically, it may be awhile before she gets over the accumulative effects of all the attempts on her life within the last couple of months.

"Thank god," exhaled Peg. "I certainly hope this is the end of it. There is not one suspect left now is there? I don't think anyway, except for . . . Alice?" she suggests when updating detectives, Marvin and Sam when they arrived.

"That is the second time you saved me. Now you can never leave my side," smiles Emma through tears, and apparently still in a slight state of shock but slowly slipping into a mild sedated state as the sedatives takes effect.

"Don't worry, I don't want to," Peg pats her forehead and strokes her unruly hair. "Honey, I'll have to comb that for you . . ." and Peg looks around for a comb.

With the room still filled with people, the sedative she has been given takes effect and an almost asleep Emma whispers. "I hope that ends the list of all those to want to do me in . . ."

Chapter Forty-Five

"For she's a Jolly good fellow, for she's a jolly good fellow . . ."

All the customers who regularly hang out in the store, and many more, were there to greet Emma a week after she got out of the hospital and returned to the bookstore. Everyone applauded as Emma stepped up to the mic to speak.

"Thank you. I thank you for your support and well wishes and for being my friends and coming into the bookstore even when one of the mystery books seem to come to life right here in the store."

"I wish to apologize to my friends and customers for the horrendous attempt on my life while you all were in the bookstore. My last wish would be to put my friends and customers in danger while they are in my store," Emma profusely apologizes then turns to look at Peg.

"My heartfelt thanks goes out to Peg for protecting everyone and saving my life that day," Emma says with tears in her eyes.

Peg so used to being at her post was standing near the door now, pipes up and says, "You can thank your customers and friends for screaming and alerting me and also startling and throwing off the perpetrator's aim." She smiled as the room clapped.

"Yes, give yourselves a hand," laughed Peg. She was coming to really enjoy this crowd.

The whole room clapped even louder upon hearing this.

Acknowledgements were given to Marie and Tammy for taking charge and had taking it upon themselves to change all the locks and the security code so Alice nor anyone else could get in the store or the apartment above the store where Emma lives and where Peg was now staying. Marie and Tammy took a bow and Peg spoke from her position near the door.

"Hey, this woman needs full time protection and I do not take my job lightly," Peg grins from ear to ear, appearing happily in love with Emma, and Emma seemingly feeling the same about Peg.

Peg has no idea where all this is going to go but she is hanging in there and plans on taking care of Emma.

But Peg cannot help wondering where Alice was hiding and she has been trying to find the time to get away and locate her.

Chapter Forty-Six

Alice is all alone and devastated. All alone, and left without anyone to turn to, she cries.

Alice had no idea that Charles and Bob were in cahoots even years back when Charles learned that Emma's parents owned prime real estate. Bob was needed to help pull Emma and Alice apart when Charles saw how chummy Emma and Alice were getting to be. Charles offered Bob a piece of the action if he ever got the property through a divorce. And it was Charles who had the small plane's electronic system rigged so it would suddenly lose altitude over the dense Peruvian forest. It was a well thought out plan. Bob's job was to work on Alice and he, more or less, contributed to that factor when he arranged that she lose her previous job then befriended her when she was down and out by offering to help set up her business conveniently near the bookstore knowing that sooner or later Alice would run into Emma.

Chapter Forty-Seven

Marvin and Sam continued their investigations and although they could not pin down anything specific, a criminal accessory-to-the-crime charge was pending on Alice. They did get her on outstanding driving violations and they were still looking for more reasons to bring her in. Alice lost her office space and immediately Penny snatched it up and extended her smoothie business in the other direction rather than trying to get the bookstore space. Penny's business continues to strive and grow, with double the space she had room to hire extra help and offer more eating space.

Alice was upset over Bob's death. An autopsy report confirmed that he was smothered and it was assumed that Charles was the murderer since he was in the building, and Bob died the same way Charles tried to kill Emma.

For what reason though, Emma knew Charles was angry because he could not get the bookstore property. The divorce judge had ruled in favor of Emma since her parents willed the store to her. Apparently Charles and Bob were swindlers and marriages to Emma and Alice were planned, because the guys thought they could use Alice to get to Emma and somehow get the property the bookstore sat on. And further investigation into Emma's parent's tragic demise was looked into and the finger points to Bob and Charles' involvement.

"But why?" asked Emma. "What was the big attraction to this bookstore that drove these men to murder?"

Marvin and Sam looked at each other, "Greed! You are sitting on a gold mine. This is prime territory for expansion. The others on the block are willing to sign but your parents were not and you were not willing to sell which messed up Bob and Charles' plans. They were getting impatient," explained Marvin.

"But you did the people who love this area a huge favor, and I believe your regular customers realized that all along. I believe your more psychic regulars like Edie and Georgette would tell us that they had a bad feeling about Charles all along."

"Marie said Tammy said that they always had a bad feeling about him, well, him and Alice," explained Sam and then went on, "Err, please don't hold that against them!"

"Well, I guess I was the only blind one then," professed Emma looking rather sheepish and down in the dumps.

"Well, love is a huge distraction, I'm sure we all can agree on that," piped up Marvin. "Yes, love is a huge distraction."

Chapter Forty-Eight

Alice seemed to have disappeared, her office was left as is, she never returned to it. Emma thinks about her but never hears from her. Emma realizes that Alice was being played by Bob and his many schemes.

After all was said and done, Emma felt very blessed to have her friends at the bookstore and Peg in her life.

****

Emma recovered nicely from her bullet wound. Physically she was healing but her nerves were bad and doctors had given her sedatives to sleep at night. She kept busy in the bookstore and was glad the open mic regulars were there. Emma gave the regulars a special discount on books, drinks and food because they brought in so many customers. They bought and read books and referred to them on open mic creating more business because more books and refreshments were sold.

Yes, open mic is very popular at the bookstore even Peg has been known to spout off a bit at the mic; her favorite topic being about global warming. She helps Emma around the bookstore too when she is not busy. There is just too much to say now and too many books to read to not mention the monetary injustices and the global power struggles. How the occupy groups are stating, "We know what is going on and for what and we think things should change in order to secure the planet for the future of our children instead of allowing short term rule of greed and power."

The world may be a mess but the small historical area of the city remains intact. No one is selling out to big time corporations but hanging onto their own individual personal small businesses, which make this wonderful area so quaint and unique and such a crowd pleaser.

The little bookstore became so famous with the attempts on Emma's life and all, that many more people come to visit the area. Business was booming and Emma was able to give everyone a raise and also turn the bookstore into a co-op.

Word got out about Frank's nephew needing a transplant and huge donations came in. He was fortunate enough to find a match and both the organ donor and Frank's nephew are doing fine.

Many stories such as this came out of all the attempts on Emma life and the pain and suffering surrounding the little bookstore. Georgette wrote a book and there is even talk of a movie.

Emma and Peg were together and doing just fine

living above the store and sharing their love of books, people and each other.

Yet Emma often thought of Alice. She came back into her life in a flash and now was gone again—in a flash. Emma missed Alice but the bookstore along with Peg was a great diversion and kept Emma occupied.

Chapter Forty-Nine

It's before work and Marvin is on his way to get yet another smoothie when he gets a call from Sam. "Hey, Marvin, I just got the information we wanted from the records department are you sitting down?"

"Yeah, in my car," answers Marvin.

"Are you at that smoothie shop? Hey bring me a strawberry smoothie, will you?" asked Sam.

"Okay, will do. What's up Sam?" Marvin asked.

"Well, it seems that the lawyer, George Dewey, drew up Emma's Revocable Trust which leaves the bookstore to Marie and Tammy upon her death and that Joe Cheater, another lawyer at the same firm represented Charles Kingston, Emma's ex-husband during his divorce and lawsuit attempts to get half of the bookstore. Does that seem odd to you that they used lawyers from the same firm? And that all this was done within a time frame of about five or less years," revealed Sam and continues on.

"I think we need to speak with Emma again,

don't you? Why don't I meet you at the smoothie shop then we'll walk around the block and not go through the bookstore but to Emma private entrance to her apartment? I don't want Tammy and Marie to see us."

****

Sam and Marvin walked around to the private entrance to Emma's apartment above the bookstore. Sam rang the bell and within minutes Emma answers the door.

"Hello Detective, is there something I can do for you?"

"Hi Emma, may we come in for a few minutes, we would like to talk with you, if this is a good time. Is Peg here too?" asked Marvin.

"No Peg is at work. Please come in." Emma motioned for them to step inside.

"Well, we are only really interested in talking to you alone anyway, Emma," Marvin smiled.

"Coffee?" Emma asked.

"No thanks, Emma we hate to bother you with you just getting out of the hospital and all, but we have a few questions to ask you that have come up during our investigation," replied Sam.

"Such as?" questions Emma.

"Well, like when you changed your will. First of all, did Alice know the beneficiary of your will?" asked Marvin.

"I think she may have thought that she was beneficiary by something I said in the hospital when that car almost hit me."

"What did you say?" Marvin was intrigued.

"Well I'm not sure why I said it, just subconsciously doubting everyone at that time. I had felt that Alice was being distant and I wanted to bring that out in her. I wanted to see her reaction when I nonchalantly said that it was a good thing that I had my will in order and something to the effect that she would be a rich woman one day if something were to happen to me."

"How did she react to that?" asked Sam.

"Well, not really in any sort of way, almost like it didn't matter, she really seemed genuinely concerned about my welfare. Why do you ask?" wondered Emma.

"Well, the lawyer you used when you changed from Alice and added Marie and Tammy to the new will, George Dewey, comes from the same firm as the lawyer, Joe Cheater. And he, if you recall, represented your ex-husband Charles during all your divorce proceedings," explained Marvin.

"Interesting." And then confused, "What?" Emma now had a worried expression and went to sit down with Marvin and Sam at the kitchen table suddenly feeling out of breath.

"So, I guess our question is, who suggested the lawyer when it was your idea to change your will and remove Alice as bookstore beneficiary and add Marie and Tammy instead?" asked Sam.

"I never changed that trust!" Emma had the look of horror on her face. "Alice is still the beneficiary to my estate," Emma said looking even more confused and troubled now. "After Alice and I got back together I changed the trust to make her the full beneficiary to my estate."

"Oh, well not according to public filing in this state at the county records office," explained Marvin.

"What?" Emma couldn't believe what she was hearing and was glad she was already sitting down. Sam searched the cabinets, found a glass and poured her a glass of water at the sink then set it down in front of her. She readily took a sip, her hand slightly shaking.

Marvin and Sam both looked at each other and said, "Don't tell me Marie, Tammy, and Charles were in cahoots?"

Emma sat dumfounded. "How can this be?"

"And that it was Charles who planted Marie, Tammy and Bob and probably Alice was ignorant of the whole ordeal and was just being used." Sam goes on, "Something doesn't make sense, were Charles and Bob working against each other? Behind each other's back?"

"But the fact remains that someone altered your Revocable Trust illegally and that makes Marie and Tammy look very suspicious," contributed Marvin.

"Come on Marvin, let's go downstairs and pay Tammy and Marie a visit," Sam was eager to get to the bottom of this. Emma merely sat there dumbfounded. This was going to take a moment to sink in.

"I'm okay, no need to call Peg," Emma said when Marvin asked. "But thanks! I'll be okay, I just need to sit here a moment and digest all of this."

After Marvin and Sam left Emma received a call from Peg checking to see how she was doing. Perfect timing, for Emma had a question she was eager to ask Peg. "Peg, I need to talk to Alice, I hope you understand."

"Are you sure you want to go over there? You'll

probably get nothing but lies," Peg tried to dissuade her.

"Well, I need to take that chance, for myself and what she and I had together. I need to find out for sure if she had anything to do with all of this," explained Emma.

"Well, you know she worked out of the same office with her husband, doesn't that in itself, make her look suspicious?" asked Peg. "Maybe I should come with you."

"No, I need to talk to her alone, I think," Emma said ending the phone call while grabbing her purse and jacket and heading out the door.

Chapter Fifty

Meanwhile back in the bookstore, Marvin corners Marie and Sam heads off Tammy and manages to corner her. It is unnoticeable to the busy customers but very noticeable by Marie and Tammy as to what was happening. Marvin and Sam managed to gather the ladies and suggested they talk in a more private location, like downtown. "Come with me ladies, we are going to take a ride downtown to headquarters."

"What? What on earth for . . . you have no right," protested Marie.

"It would be better, don't you think, if you came peacefully?" suggested Sam gesturing the ladies towards the door.

The ladies went along willingly alerting store workers on the way out the door. Upon arrival at headquarters, Marvin and Sam put the ladies into separate interrogating rooms, Marvin took Marie and Sam headed Tammy into another room where each twosome could speak in private.

"What big book store chain did you work for, Marie?" pressured Marvin.

"Why, International Books, what does that have to do with anything, detective?" returned Marie with a cock of her head and a smirk on her lips.

"International Books?" Marvin repeated. "Aren't they one of the big chains who have pressured Emma to sell her bookstore? And didn't they really put the pressure on right about six years ago, after Emma's parents died? Interesting how suddenly you and Tammy show up here from another city looking for a job at this particular independent bookstore."

"Tammy and I were sick of big corporate bureaucracy and wanted and needed a change of pace, a change of scenery, a new start," explained Marie.

"Is that what Charles told you to say, if asked?" demanded Marvin.

"What are you talking about? I just came here for a job."

"Well, my partner and I have been doing some investigating and we find that the lawyers you, Tammy and Charles used came from the same firm. A firm known to represent big corporations."

"So?" questioned Marie.

"So, well just so happens, their biggest client is International Books."

"So?" Marie questioned again.

"Could it be that the lawyers were offering Charles a big cut, and Charles got Bob on board thinking Alice was in the will and in the meantime another lawyer fixed the documents to make you and Tammy beneficiaries, sealing up the whole deal?"

****

At the same time in the other room, Sam was pressuring Tammy, who claimed to know nothing and said she was pleading the Fifth. She only volunteered that she knew their names were on the documents listed as beneficiaries in Emma's will when Sam reminded her that her and Marie's signatures matched those on some of the documents proving they were involved in the fraud and that this pertinent evidence would hold up nicely in a court of law.

"Now, Tammy, if you two cooperate with me, perhaps you and I can work a deal so sentencing goes lighter for you. Perhaps if this is your first offense, the judge will go easy on you with little to no jail time and maybe only community service," he lied. He was not really supposed to do that but, the hell with it, he thought.

Tammy shot back, "I demand to talk to my attorney!"

"You mean George Dewey, the one who drew up the new fraudulent trust, or Charles' attorney, Joe Cheater?"

"I'm not saying anything until I can talk to George Dewey."

"And why is that, Tammy?" Sam asked. "Because he is the one who counseled you about the trust?"

"Okay, thank you then Tammy for just now confessing that you know about the fraudulent trust," Sam was relieved. "And I now place you under arrest."

"Wait, Emma was in on that?" demanded Tammy.

"I'm afraid Emma will not concur, we spoke to

Emma and she knows nothing of a trust handing things over to you and Marie," assured Sam. "You madam, are under arrest," and he begins to read Tammy the Miranda rights.

"Well, it was Marie's idea," Tammy stood her ground.

"You do know that I am recording this interview and it will be used in a court of law? An attorney will be appointed for you and in this case you cannot use either George Dewy or Joe Cheater or any other lawyer associated with that firm. For those two chaps are being gathered up right now as we speak. They are in a heap of trouble too," declared Sam.

"So, I thank you Tammy for being most cooperative, tell me who all was in on this? You, Marie, Charles, Bob, and Alice?"

"Alice was not in on this, she was unaware. Remember, you said if I cooperate, the judge will give me a break." Tammy looking stressed now continued, "Alice was supposed to be a victim, and the property would then go to Bob."

"I am so sick of all of this. The thing wasn't my idea. I've been a wreck. I got roped into this," Tammy was near tears now.

"The DA is on his way over, he'll work with you. So Tammy, what you are telling me is that Charles and Bob were working against each other. So it was Charles' plan all along to eliminate Bob and get him out of the picture? But, with the trust fraudulently changed, he didn't have to kill Bob, just Emma?" Sam was puzzled. "That doesn't make sense?"

Tammy tearfully explained what she thought she knew about it all anyway.

"Bob was getting too sloppy. He wasn't getting rid of Emma fast enough. Bob hired that hit man who kept messing things up. I was the go between. Charles had me tell Bob to bump off Emma, and to hurry it up. He wanted to tell me how he was going to do it . . . I just . . . I didn't want to hear about it. I told him."

Tammy was now getting all upset and sweating profusely.

"The whole idea came from Charles and Marie," confessed Tammy.

"So, things between Alice and Emma, went sour because Alice went back to her husband, Bob?" Sam dug deeper.

Tammy tried to explain, "Bob offered Alice a position in his office, he was really the backbone, financier for her getting that location, in a 'let's be friends way,' he offered that to her to keep an eye on her. He hoped to learn more about Emma that way or so, he assumed that Alice was the beneficiary of the bookstore if anything should happen to Emma. He wasn't in love with her."

Suddenly Tammy begins to sob . . . "He was in love with me!" She covered her face and burst into tears.

"What? Whoa! Wait, now I am really confused." Sam was becoming more bewildered.

Tammy went on to explain, "Charles and Bob were partners; we all worked for International Books in one capacity or another. The deal was taking too long, things needed to speed up because other large firms were becoming interested. We had to get the property so International Books could deal with us.

"If you don't mind me asking?" said Sam. "What about Marie?"

"Well, truth be told Marie and I are not the twins everyone thinks we are."

"Interesting." *This is too wild,* thought Sam. *I think I need to retire.*

Chapter Fifty-One

Alice sat in her apartment, now all alone and crying, with arrest being threatened, waiting charges after further investigation. She sits and thinks about her past, her childhood, her marriage to Bob and how he tricked her. She tries to keep busy with routine household cleaning chores, but while mopping the hardwood floor in the living room she suddenly bursts into tears and had to sit down and sob.

She thought about Emma and how she truly loved her and missed her terribly. She knows all is lost and that Emma is with Peg now.

There are no second chances, she learned that as a kid and love is not for her. People do not give you a second chance. She realized Bob played her for a fool, offering a cool position, planting her right near Emma's bookstore knowing sooner rather than later they would reunite. It was Bob who years earlier shamed shy conservative Alice away from her relationship with Emma, and then now comes into her life and uses her by helping her get reunited just so she could get information for him. He knew Emma and I were together once again and that I was named in the will. He knew all of this, all along. I am such a fool.

I wonder how did he did know? Did he just assume? Or was there help? Maybe someone who has easy access to public records, if not, knew someone who did.

Peg sure jumped in on the scene quick and nice and easy!

Alice begins to cry again at the thought of Emma with Peg. Oh this is so bad, of course I want to blame someone when it was me, who really messed things up with Emma.

And sitting there all alone, she continues to cry.

Suddenly, there is a knock at the door. Alice is startled and gets up to grab a tissue out of the box on the bookshelf behind the door, to wipe her tears before looking through the peek hole to see who is knocking at her door.

She hears a familiar voice say, "It's Emma!"

Alice can't believe that Emma is at her door and starts to shake with worry. This can't be good she thinks. Emma must think that I am behind everything that has happened.

She is shaking as she peeps through the peep hole a second time and it appears that Emma is alone.

"Come on Alice, let me in. I want to talk," Emma pleas.

Worried and visibly upset, Alice slowly opens the door and a teary eyed Emma stands there looking about as dreadful as she herself looks.

"What are you doing here?" asked Alice.

"Can I come in? I think we need to talk and clear up a few things," suggested Emma, as she entered Alice's apartment.

"Okay come in." Alice steps aside and opens the door wider to let Emma step past her into her living-room. She closes the door but not before taking another quick look outside making sure Emma is indeed alone. She can't believe that Emma came alone to talk. She thought for sure either Peg or the two detectives would be with her. Shaking slightly she slowly closes the door behind her.

"Alice, sit!" demands Emma in a soft voice.

"Okay, I'm sitting," says Alice. Emma sits down too.

"Now, let's go back in time, and tell me everything you know," demands Emma.

"All I know is that awhile back, out of the blue Bob called, we chatted he said he had moved on, he was sorry he never gotten around to signing the divorce papers and said that he would. We chatted on and during the course of the conversation I mentioned I could use more business. He was friendly enough, well at one point a little too flirty. I said I'd have none of that. He agreed and backed off, and said just friends then. He then suggested that I work with him. He offered me a position as a consultant in his new business. He said he had a position to fill and I needed more work until my business built-up, and knowing my background, said I would be perfect. I was down and out, my money was running low. I thought well okay then, just for a while and I wanted to make sure the divorce papers got finalized,"admitted Alice. And she continued.

"And so yes, he help set me up with a job, that part you knew, what you didn't know is that he dragged his feet concerning the divorce papers. And now I realized why he did. He thought that I was in your will!" Alice went on.

"I had no idea that he was in on a scam with Charles. I swear," pleads Alice. "I guess if he thought that I was in your will, and we were still married then . . ."

Alice was interrupted then by Emma. "Alice, you were next in line to be murdered, after me, that is unless…" explained Emma.

"No wonder he never signed those divorce papers. He was using me to get his hands on your property."

"Exactly, unless . . ." Emma agreed.

Alice presses on. "Emma, I swear that I wasn't in on it. I didn't know you had me in your will. It didn't matter to me, you have to believe me."

"But you had sex with him," Emma sounded upset.

"Actually, I know I made it sound that way in order to make you jealous," Alice confessed.

Emma gave her a stern look. Alice caught it and quickly went on, "You were shunning me, I thought we were over. You were coming home later and later so I worked longer and longer hours. We should have talked. I should have talked."

"I should have talked too," Emma quietly said.

"Actually, and I so realize this now, Bob was using my dumb silly ass to get to you. I was a fool!" Alice was connecting the dots and beginning to see the light.

They were both quiet then and maybe even feeling a little uncomfortable. The silence was deafening. Then Alice had a sudden thought and piped up, however nervously, quickly asked. "So, how's, Peg?" Alice asked but to herself thought *I thought perhaps with all this going on she never let you out of her sight.* But kept that remark inside admitting to herself that it might have sounded rude and argumentative and she just didn't have it in her to go there. She was too worn out.

"I told her I wanted to come alone today to speak to you," said Emma.

That deafening yet screaming silence was back again as they sat facing each other, Emma on the couch and Alice opposite in a chair near the door.

Emma sat for a moment taking in all the sudden shifts in events. Trying to sort things out and come to terms with all the deceit that has been going on. Okay, so it seems that Tammy and Marie are the only ones left to benefit from her death now and they for sure by now were in custody. No one knew this but herself.

"I appreciate you coming to speak with me. I'm sorry that I hurt you. I have no idea what was going through my brain. Maybe I'm just the kind of person that cannot accept being loved. Maybe I don't know how to love. I know I realize what a wonderful thing I have after I have pushed it away and then it's too late." Alice was pouring out her heart.

And went on, "Yes, I was helping Bob and I knew he wanted you to sell the bookstore. I messed up big time. I had no idea he would stoop to murder. How dumb am I?" Alice was near tears again.

"I was next on the hit list; now I know why he never signed those divorce papers he stood to gain everything. He used me! I am so naïve!" Alice began to cry softly.

"Oh stop beating yourself up; neither one of us is dead," Emma said half jokingly, half not.

"I wonder who knew that you were cut out of the will Alice, and that Tammy and Marie replaced you? You didn't know?" Alice shook her head in denial, with tears running down her cheeks, got up to get a tissue. Emma continues on with her thoughts.

"Bring me a tissue too will you please? Of course, Tammy and Marie knew. So someone has to still bump me off to gain everything. Charles is dead Bob is dead. Who is going to do the deed?" Emma wondered out loud.

No sooner had she asked the question, and her answer burst through the apartment door, kicking it wide, charging in, with revolver held out in front of her with both hands, police style. Peg pointed the gun at Emma sitting directing in front of her.

"You? Peg? You? Why you? What do you have to gain?" shocked, Emma managed to ask. Emma sat frozen in fear.

"Silly detectives you have on board, neither one ever thought to check that I was new on the force, straight from a security job at International Books and conveniently married to your ex. Charles and the others offered me a deal that I couldn't refuse and a chance to relocate and meet new and wonderful people, and get all expenses paid. They even had political pull in your police department by way of some people at the top and some fancy lawyers. All planned out to have me assigned to personally protect you, which, of course in the end, enabled me to conveniently kill off my competition when the time was right. Yes, I'm part of the partnership with Charles, Marie and Tammy," confessed Peg.

"What? You're married to Charles!" Emma was in shock.

Peg confesses everything then cocks her gun to get ready to pull the trigger. But, Peg, so busy bragging about being married to Charles and being part of the scheme had let her guard down. She had forgotten about Alice. Where was Alice? Peg only saw Emma. Peg's big mistake! Alice had just gotten up to get a tissue out of the box on the bookshelf behind the open door; she was now silently standing in the shadows behind Peg. Carefully Alice grabbed the nearby cleaning mop she had luckily left propped there earlier, and swung it at Peg's gun to throw off Peg's aim or knock it out of her hand, just as Peg saw Alice from the corner of her eye. Too late! Alice's swing of the long mop handle was hard and strong and made clean contact, knocking the gun out of Peg's hands and on to the floor. In a nanosecond before Peg realized what had happened, Alice flew to the floor pushing the gun over towards Emma. Emma like a flash went for it and snatched it up, holding it firmly in both hands as Alice pulled out her cell phone and called the police.

Within a few minutes, officers along with detectives Sam and Marvin were at Alice's apartment. Peg was wrong; Sam and Marvin did not forget to check Peg's records and personal file. They found that she was newly hired and was a security officer at International Books, still on the payroll there. And the lawyers, George Dewey and Joe Cheater had influence in the department, and were in on the planning.

****

The police had Marie, Tammy, Peg, and the lawyers in custody and certain officials in the police department were being investigated.

Marvin and Sam had bonuses coming for their extraordinary detective work.

"Sam, just think of all the smoothies we can buy with that extra pay. Let's get one now to celebrate," suggested Marvin.

"You're on!" smiled Sam.

****

All the commotion was over. The police were gone. Peg was gone. The police took her away in handcuffs. Alice and Emma found themselves, standing on the front steps at Alice's apartment building she had just moved into.

"Looks like we're the only two left!" smiled Emma. "Looks like I could use some help in the bookstore. Since I just lost two of my employees."

"And I have no job!" smiled Alice.

Emma looked around. "It's quiet here," she finally said.

"The twists and turns our lives have taken. Well, we survived and we are on a new path now." Emma continued, "Well, no matter how rotten Charles and Bob were, they brought us together twice." Alice pointed out and Emma agreed.

Just then two young women in their twenties walked by arm in arm and obviously in love.

212

"Wow, can you imagine! We never would have done that!" smiled Alice.

"Yeah, we couldn't even bring ourselves to say the word lesbian."

"You know, I might have to do a ten minute open mic myself and talk about the slow change of the church and subsequent snails pace of social change. It's all so silly isn't it when you really think about it."

And Alice had to agree smiling, "I'm glad we had 'us'." Then Alice stood with tears in her eyes and said. "Well, it may be quiet here but I miss 'us' and our simple way of life we had before all of this came down on us."

"I miss us too," smiled Emma. "Did you sign the lease already?" Emma asked smiling, feeling flirty and swinging her long silvery white hair over her shoulder, some strands drifting down framing her perfectly smooth olive complexion.

Alice stood quietly for a moment just smiling, tears in her eyes. She loved it when Emma flirted. Then suddenly as if she couldn't contain herself any longer she threw her head back as if tossing fate to the wind.

"Yes I did, but. The hell with the lease . . ." Emma's flirting always worked wonders with Alice, she was dead serious about not caring about the lease; with a smile she flew into Emma's arms, right there on the street, in public for all the world to see, on the cobblestone side walk near the neatly trimmed hedge and street lined with lovely maple trees.

They kissed then on the lips in public. They have come a long way. Both of them! They stood for a second just standing there arms around each other looking into each other's eyes. There really were no words, no need for words. It was just time to go home.

"Come on, let's walk home," Emma smiled.

And down the sidewalk they walked, arm in arm. Smiling.

About the Author

Dianne Zimmermann lives in St. Louis and *Emma's Run* is her first novel. When she isn't writing she enjoys running, bicycling and drawing.